M000313500

ANSWER
THE Call

**DISCOVER
LIFE'S
PURPOSE**

ANSWER
THE Call

**DISCOVER
LIFE'S
PURPOSE**

WARREN
HENDERSON

All Scripture quotations are from the New King James Version of the Bible, unless otherwise noted. Copyright © 1982 by Thomas Nelson, Inc. Nashville, TN

Answer the Call
By Warren Henderson
Copyright © 2009

Published by Gospel Folio Press
304 Killaly Street West
Port Colborne, ON, L3K 6A6, Canada

ISBN 978-1-897117-89-7

ORDERING INFORMATION:
Gospel Folio Press
Phone 1-905-835-9166
E-mail: order@gospelfolio.com

Printed in the Canada

Table of Contents

Acknowledgements

The author is indebted to all those who contributed to the publishing of *Answer the Call.* I praise the Lord Jesus Christ and thank Him for each of the following individuals and for their contributions: Randy Amos, Mike Attwood, David Dunlap, and Jack Spender for technical editing. Kathleen Henderson for general editing. Matthew Henderson and David Lindstrom for proofreading assistance.

Preface

On December 23, 1806 Beethoven's Violin Concerto in D major, Opus 61 premiered at the Theater an der Wien in Vienna. The novelty of the opening measure was so unanticipated that many in the audience questioned whether the musical composition had actually begun. There was no initial chord or gigantic unison, nothing but four soft beats on the timpani. Until Beethoven's time, the drum, the lowliest member of the orchestra, had rarely been used in such a notable expression, especially as a solo instrument. Again and again the four beats are heard throughout the arrangement, creating a superb effect.

What inspired Ludwig van Beethoven's concerto? The idea was suggested to him after hearing repeated knocking at a neighbor's door in the stillness of the night.[1] Continued knocking at the door meant that no one was responding to the visitor's summons; either it had not been heard or it was being ignored. In the same way that many listeners misunderstood the repeated knocking within Beethoven's concerto, many more today are oblivious to God's calling for their lives or are choosing to ignore His beckoning.

God is summoning every man, woman, and child to be a part of His eternal purposes. Whether or not we hear God calling depends on the openness of our ears; whether or not we answer the call depends on the yielding condition of our heart. Nowhere in Scripture does God constrain anyone to surrender against their will. He kindly invites, graciously petitions, and mercifully warns, but He does not force Himself on anyone. As Lord of all, and Creator of all, He certainly is able to interject His will into

1

ours, but then our actions become robotic gestures lacking the luster of love. We demonstrate adoration for God by obeying His calling and commands (John 14:15).

God speaks to His children in the quietness of His presence, but each believer is free to depart from this privileged realm of communion to go his or her own way. Adam chose to follow his wife in rebellion rather than to do what he knew was right; consequently, casual strolls with the Lord in the morning air were no longer possible. Cain chose to murder his righteous brother Abel, rather than to submit to God's prescribed way of worship; he was banished from God's presence to wander aimlessly upon the earth. Jonah determined to escape to Joppa and put out to sea rather than to preach God's message to hostile Nineveh as commanded. God did not force Jonah to submit to His will, but He did put Jonah in such a desperate situation that Jonah wished he had obeyed. From the belly of a huge fish Jonah repented of his sin and at that moment divine communion was restored. Accordingly, freely-reciprocated love, founded in truth, will always be the essence of God-accepted worship and fellowship with Him (John 4:23-24).

The irresistible love of God can only be experienced by answering His invitation to know Him. Our understanding of God's plan and our commitment to live it out will be directly proportional to the extent that we have known and experienced Him. The Lord Jesus said, *"He who has My commandments and keeps them, it is he who loves Me. And he who loves Me will be loved by My Father, and I will love him and manifest Myself to him"* (John 14:21). Continued submission to divine truth is the pathway to intimately experiencing and knowing God in deepening degrees. It is this consistent contact with God's nature that results in our comprehension of His wondrous design for our lives. Oswald Chambers summarizes:

> My contact with the nature of God will shape my understanding of His call and will help me realize what I truly desire to do for Him. The call of God is an expression of His nature; the

service which results in my life is suited to me and is an expression of my nature. ... Service is the overflow which pours from a life filled with love and devotion. ... Service is what I bring to the relationship and is the reflection of my identification with the nature of God. Service becomes a natural part of my life. God brings me into the proper relationship with Himself so that I can understand His call, and then I serve Him on my own out of a motivation of absolute love. Service to God is the deliberate love-gift of a nature that has heard the call of God. Service is an expression of my nature, and God's call is an expression of His nature.[2]

Are you consistently having close encounters with the Lord? Do you hear His still, quiet voice as you mediate on His Word and petition Him in prayer? If not, it is time to take action – it is time to respond to His invitation. God desires your presence and is inviting you to have contact and communion with Him. The extent to which we respond to this invitation and have contact with God's nature will ultimately determine our wherewithal to know God, to express His nature to others, and to adhere to His calling for our lives.

Is God Calling Me?

Many have contemplated this question, some have agonized over it. "Is God calling me to the mission field or to a particular ministry?" "Is God calling me to marry a particular individual or to remain single?" Before identifying the types of divine calls, a biblical understanding of the nature of God's call itself is necessary. Generally speaking, our concept of "the call of God" does not reflect the Greek grammar of the New Testament. It is not God's ongoing call that is the main focus of Scripture, but rather the fulfillment of what He has already called to be which is paramount.

The Greek grammar of the New Testament Epistles provides some clues in understanding the mysterious nature of God's call. Observations include:

1. The word "calling" is normally rendered from *kelsis* (a noun); the verb form is never used to speak of an active calling of God.
2. The "called" of God either refers to the *keltos* (a noun associated with those called or appointed of God for something) or *kaleo* (a verb speaking of that which God has determined to be). *Kaleo* is usually in the aorist indicative, meaning God has already called. Thus, His initial call is immutable and is affirmed in time.
3. The word "calls" occurs only four times in the epistles (Rom. 4:17, 9:11; Gal. 5:7-8; 1 Thess. 5:23-24) and relates to the believer's calling in Christ. In these instances, *kaleo* is an active verbal adjective. The

5

rarity of an *active* divine calling seems to highlight the significances of God's sovereign purpose in time as determined by His foreknowledge.

In summary, the usages of *kaleo*, *keltos*, and *kelsis* show the incomprehensible and timeless union of God's sovereign design and foreknowledge in relationship with the outworking of human responsibility. Paul acknowledges the timeless aspect of God's calling by saying, *"God ...calls those things which do not exist as though they did"* (Rom. 4:17) and *"He who calls you is faithful, who also will do it"* (1 Thess. 5:24). Time does not hold or constrain God's actions, but He does unfold and work out His sovereign plan in time. What He has "called" is based on His foreknowledge and predetermined counsel.

Before creation, God previewed the corridors of time, considered all the possible permutations of natural cause and effect as well as the future choices of cognitive beings, and made sovereign choices to bless humanity in time and glorify His name throughout time and eternity. As only a triune God existed when the plan of redemption was devised, the plan is solely His – it originated in His mind and He deserves all the glory for it. God's choices ensure that humanity will receive the greatest possible blessing and that He will obtain the most glory as a result.

The apostles wrote of both the timeless call of God and our responsibility to obey His call:

Paul writes:
The divine call: *"I, therefore, the prisoner of the Lord, beseech you to walk worthy of the calling with which you were called"* (Eph 4:1).

Human responsibility to answer the call: *"For we are His workmanship, created in Christ Jesus for good works, which God prepared beforehand that we should walk in them"* (Eph. 2:10).

Peter writes:
The divine call: *"Elect according to the foreknowledge of God the Father"* (1 Pet. 1:2).

Human responsibility to answer the call: *"Therefore, brethren, be even more diligent to make your call and election sure, for if you do these things you will never stumble"* (2 Pet. 1:10).

John writes:
The divine call: *"I have set before you an open door, and no one can shut it"* (Rev. 3:9).

Human responsibility to answer the call: *"Hold fast what you have, that no one may take your crown"* (Rev. 3:11).

These seemingly contradictory aspects of God's call create an intentional dichotomy in the human brain. Incomplete answers to our inadequate questions do not satisfy our inquiring minds, but these incomprehensible aspects of God's calling do prompt our awe of God and our humility before Him. There are some matters man is not expected to understand; in these abstruse areas of reality being dumbfounded is the expected and God-honoring outcome (Deut. 29:29). Logically speaking, a time-dependent being cannot fully understand time-independent truth – the tie between creation order and the ultimate eternal order of things rests solely in God's resolve to complete His predetermined counsel.

Concerning our divine calling, one cannot read Scripture without marveling at divine wisdom and design, yet each of God's calls had to be personally obeyed. In a manner that we cannot fully understand, human responsibility and sovereign design are intimately connected in God's plan for our lives. Such a realization is proof that we cannot obtain divinity, nor should we seek to. Unfortunately, the systemization of Scripture in these perplexing matters has caused some Christians to overstate what Scripture actually teaches, others to superficially accept God's Word, and many more to just ignore the matter of God's calling altogether. The best response is to state what Scripture says and leave the unrevealed details with the Lord.

Man has no choice in being a part of God's plan, but as a moral and a conscious being, he has every choice in how he will answer God's call and be used within God's unfolding design. Whether or not we yield to His call, God will be glorified through our choices; He will use us either as vessels of mercy prepared for glory, or as vessels of wrath fit for destruction (Rom. 9:14-23). God prepares yielded vessels for glory and re-bellious vessels to receive His wrath.

For example, God did not force Pharaoh to worship Egyptian gods, but He did intervene to harden Pharaoh's heart on certain occasions to accomplish the release of His people from Egypt. The fact that Pharaoh hardened his own heart afterwards demonstrates he still had free-choice in the matter. God would have been perfectly just to destroy a pagan like Pharaoh, but instead He designed ten specific plagues to prove to Pharaoh that He was superior to a number of specific Egyptian gods. Pharaoh rejected this revelation and hardened his own heart against the Lord – he prepared himself to be a vessel of wrath fit for destruction. God brought glory to His name by honoring Pharaoh's decision, which God already foreknew. This example shows how human responsibility and sovereign design ensure that God will receive all the glory in every situation.

When God first summoned Moses to deliver His people from bondage and from Egypt, Moses rejected the idea. He argued that the Israelites would not believe that he was from God, that the Egyptians would not release their slave force, and that, beside all this, he was not an eloquent speaker. A few moments later, after God demonstrated His power and affirmed Aaron as his helper, Moses surrendered to God's call with complete devotion. The Greek word *therapon*, translated "servant" in Hebrews 3:5, is used to describe the type of servant Moses was. *Therapon* is not the typical word used in the New Testament to describe a servant or a slave. This word conveys the idea of a voluntary servant who is motivated by devotion for his superior. At first, Moses was hesitant to accept the call of God for his life, but when he did, he did so of his own free will because he loved the Lord.

Is God calling you? Absolutely. His personal call for you was initiated long before your conception; in fact, God was mindful of you before the foundations of the world were laid. The prophet Isaiah wrote, *"The Lord has called Me from the womb; from the matrix of My mother He has made mention of My name"* (Isa. 49:1). While commissioning a young Jeremiah as a prophet, God said, *"Before I formed you in the womb I knew you; Before you were born I sanctified you; I ordained you a prophet to the nations"* (Jer. 1:5). Jeremiah, after hearing these words, asserted that he was too young to fulfill God's calling for his life. But after further divine encouragement, Jeremiah chose to obey God's call and became an emboldened mouthpiece for God during one of the most distressing eras of Jewish history. In the autumn years of his life, he would pen the second longest book in the Bible.

The profound nature of God's call for each of our lives demands our utmost reverence and respect as each one seeks to know and obey His will. His ways are above our ways. His thoughts are above our thoughts. The ultimate experience in life is to know God and to serve Him in the way He has deemed best. Only then does the spirit of man find what it longs for – joyful fellowship with God.

Oh, the depth of the riches both of the wisdom and knowledge of God! How unsearchable are His judgments and His ways past finding out! "For who has known the mind of the LORD? Or who has become His counselor?" "Or who has first given to Him and it shall be repaid to him?" For of Him and through Him and to Him are all things, to whom be glory forever. Amen (Rom. 11:33-36).

A Promotion Offer

"Promotion" is one of those words that excites just about everyone, regardless of their occupation. Whether a soldier gains a higher rank or an employee advances in position, promotions are welcomed events. The intended purpose of God's calling is to promote man into a higher spiritual status than he previously had. In short, answering God's call always results in a promotion of some sort.

Scripture reveals three general types of divine calls to humanity. Each call is timeless, but is either answered or ignored by individuals who are constrained by time. The three general calls of God to man pertain to *salvation, sanctification*, and *service*. Sometimes the Bible records the specific responses of individuals to these distinct calls. For example, Acts 16 records the conversion story of the Philippian jailer; he answered the call of salvation. Some of the Corinthian men were committing fornication with temple prostitutes; Paul commanded them to sanctify their temples (their individual bodies) unto the Lord, which they apparently did (1 Cor. 6:13-20). The book of Titus describes the type of ministry that Titus was to engage in on the island of Crete – he answered the call to service. In the case of Timothy, Paul's spiritual son, the response to all three divine calls is recorded in Scripture.

As the call to salvation is the beginning point of understanding the call of God in our lives, it will be explained first. The call to *sanctification* and the call to *service* are summarized in this chapter, but are further examined in subsequent chapters.

Salvation

It did not take long after man's appearance in Eden for him to seek independence from God and humanity has been rebelling against God ever since. Apart from God, our heart is desperately wicked (Jer. 17:9). Corruption and immoral behavior are consistent manifestations of our fallen nature which we inherited from Adam (Rom. 5:12). Therefore, without God's intervention and remedy for sin we have no hope of having our sins forgiven, no means of rightly controlling our flesh, and no mediator to restore us to a holy God. Naturally speaking, we are out of control and a lost race.

What is the Bible's central message of salvation? It can best be summarized by a short Old Testament verse which is quoted and explained three times in the New Testament: *"And he (Abram) believed in the Lord, and He accounted it to him for righteousness"* (Gen. 15:6). In this verse, the words "believed," "counted/accounted," and "righteousness" are mentioned for the first time in the Bible. This was by design, in order to limit human confusion concerning the matter of salvation. At various junctures throughout the human timeline, God would reveal a particular truth to man, without physical evidence, and hold him accountable to obey it. If an individual chose to rise above their natural senses and intellect to exercise faith in that which could not be proven, God would respond by imputing a standing (a position) of righteousness to that individual's account. This could justly be accomplished because an innocent, righteous substitute named Jesus Christ, God's own Son, took our place in judgment and suffered for all human crimes against God (Heb. 2:9; 1 Jn. 2:2; Rom. 3:25).

What is the message of salvation that must be believed today in order to receive a full pardon from God? It is that the Lord Jesus Christ, the eternal Son of God, suffered for my sins, died in my place, was buried, and arose from the dead that I might be justified and have eternal life in Him. This is called the "gospel" (literally, a "good news" message) of Jesus Christ and Paul

12

reminds the Corinthian believers that this was the very message he preached to them:

> *Moreover, brethren, I declare to you the gospel which I preached to you, which also you received and in which you stand, by which also you are saved, if you hold fast that word which I preached to you -- unless you believed in vain. For I delivered to you first of all that which I also received: that Christ died for our sins according to the Scriptures, and that He was buried, and that He rose again the third day according to the Scriptures* (1 Cor. 15:1-4).

The message of God's salvation is not exclusive in its application, for it is offered to anyone who will believe it (Rev. 22:17); it is exclusive in nature, for trusting in any other message brings eternal judgment (Gal. 1:6-9). God is *"not willing that any should perish but that all should come to repentance"* (2 Peter 3:9), but a seeking sinner must trust Christ and Him alone for his or her salvation.

The Lord Jesus extends an invitation to all who understand their miserable spiritual condition and desire to find rest for their souls by being reconciled with God. While on earth, He proclaimed, *"Come to Me, all you who labor and are heavy laden, and I will give you rest"* (Matt. 10:28) and *"He who hears My word and believes in Him who sent Me has everlasting life, and shall not come into judgment, but has passed from death into life"* (John 5:24). Concerning the Lord Jesus, Peter declared: *"Nor is there salvation in any other, for there is no other name under heaven given among men by which we must be saved"* (Acts 4:12). Paul stated, *"There is one God and one Mediator between God and men, the Man Christ Jesus, who gave Himself a ransom for all"* (1 Tim. 2:5-6).

The solution to sin is found in Christ alone; we must repent and receive Him as Saviour. A true believer will seek to practically enthrone Christ as Lord of his or her life because He is Lord over all. Repentance is the first step a sinner must take and without it there can be no salvation. The Lord Jesus said, *"Unless you repent you will all likewise perish"* (Luke 13:3). Repentance means, firstly, that you agree with God that you are a sinner deserving His judgment and that you turn away from all that you ever thought would earn you heaven; such repentance indicates a deep grief over personal sin and a desire to turn from wickedness (Jer. 8:6). Secondly, you must turn to something – that is, you must believe the gospel of Jesus Christ. For example, the Thessalonians turned to God from paganism. Their salvation was evident in that they diligently served the living and true God even while being severely persecuted for their faith (1 Thess. 1:5-9).

Likewise, Timothy had trusted Christ for salvation; thus, Paul exhorts him to live out the call of salvation that he had already answered: *"Fight the good fight of faith, lay hold on eternal life, to which you were also called and have confessed the good confession in the presence of many witnesses"* (1 Tim. 6:12). He was not only to come to Christ for salvation, but he was to go on with Christ in life. Timothy was to live out his calling in Christ with unfeigned devotion and service.

Before anyone can possibly know how he or she is to serve God, he or she must be brought into a right relationship with God. An individual must have a personal encounter with God by yielding to God's revealed Word. The *God of Glory* revealed Himself to a pagan named Abram (later named Abraham) in Ur before offering him a covenant promise. Abram's faith in God's Word was evident; he left his home and his kindred, and ventured nearly a thousand miles to serve the *God of Glory* whom he had only met once. God did not reveal Himself again to Abram until he arrived in Canaan as a pilgrim and stranger. Abraham's faith was demonstrated by his obedience and service to God (Jas. 2:17).

While fleeing to Paddanaram, the Word of the Lord came to Jacob in a dream. Though Jacob had certainly heard of the Lord, he did not know him personally, so God introduced Himself as the God of Abraham and Isaac, and then confirmed with him the covenant He had made with his grandfather Abraham. To enjoy the blessings of this covenant Jacob would have to return to Canaan, which he did some twenty years later. Like Abraham, Jacob's faith was demonstrated through obedience to God's commands.

Before Moses was sent to Egypt to deliver the Israelites from slavery, he had an encounter with God at a burning bush that was not consumed by the fire. Moses did not know the Lord until God informed Him that He was the God of Abraham, Isaac, and Jacob, then Moses feared and hid His face. Moses obeyed the Lord and by faith ventured into Egypt to deliver God's people from bondage.

A zealous Pharisee named Saul, while traveling to Damascus to persecute the Church, was overcome by a brilliant light from heaven. The Lord Jesus identified Himself and spoke to Saul from heaven. From his prostrate position on the ground Saul acknowledged Jesus Christ as Lord and then went to Damascus to await further instructions, just as he had been told to do. True faith is shown by obedience to the revealed will of God.

Have you had a close encounter with God? Have you obeyed His salvation call? It is not likely that He will speak audibly to you face to face, or from a blinding heavenly light, or in a dream, but through His Spirit He does speak directly to your heart by His Word. The Holy Spirit enables lost souls to understand and believe God's gospel message of salvation (1 Cor. 2:13-14). Without being saved you cannot do a single thing to please God, for all of our so-called *good works* apart from Christ only offend God (Isa. 64:6; Titus 1:16). If you have not trusted Christ as Saviour, why not answer His call right now – this is the first step in being used to fulfill God's eternal purpose for your life.

Isaiah had a close encounter with God. In a vision, Isaiah saw the Lord sitting upon His heavenly throne and seraphim flying about the throne declaring the holiness of God. The entire glorious scene overwhelmed Isaiah and made him keenly aware of his sinful condition before God. He said, *"Woe is me, for I am undone! Because I am a man of unclean lips"* (Isa. 6:5). Immediately, upon Isaiah's declaration, one of the seraphim took a live coal from off the altar and put it upon Isaiah's lips to purge his iniquity (Isa. 6:7). When the holiness of God's throne is realized the only solution is the mercy found at God's altar; thankfully, the Lord Jesus Christ is the believer's altar where sins can be purged and forgiven (Heb. 13:10).

With his sins purged, Isaiah was ready to seek the will of God in service. But God did not specifically address the call to Isaiah; Isaiah overheard God saying, *"Whom shall I send, and who will go for us?"* The call of God is not for the special few; it is for everyone who will hear and obey it. *"Who will go for us?"* is not a question in which God singled out Isaiah. God did not say to Isaiah, "Now go for us." There was no arm-twisting or compulsion; Isaiah was in the presence of God and when he overheard God's call, he realized that there was nothing else for him to do but to say, *"Here am I! Send me."*

After the disciples knew who the Lord Jesus was, there was simply no other right response to the Lord's kind invitation, "follow Me," than to follow Him. Close encounters with the nature of God prepare our hearts to respond to His call of service. Without personally knowing God, you will not be prompted to sincerely say, "Here am I! Send me."

Sanctification

The divine work of sanctification begins in the believer's life immediately after he or she answers the call of salvation. God begins to fashion the new believer into a holy vessel and each believer is exhorted to cooperate in the working out of what He is working into his or her life (1 Thess. 5:23; Heb. 13:21). All believers will ultimately be conformed to the moral image of Christ (Rom. 8:29); there is no human choice in that aspect of sanctification – it is God's will and power that accomplishes this. Yet, there is an ongoing call to each believer not to resist God's working in his or her life, but instead to be yielded to

Him. God promises to chasten those who choose not to submit to Him that they may be brought to a yielded position and experience sanctification (Heb. 12:6). Consequently, sanctification in a practical sense is happening to every believer, but some are more serious about it than others and, accordingly, will reap a greater blessing of being further refined now. Paul implores the Christians at Rome to yield to God's ongoing call of sanctification:

> *I beseech you therefore, brethren, by the mercies of God, that you present your bodies a living sacrifice, holy, acceptable to God, which is your reasonable service. And do not be conformed to this world, but be transformed by the renewing of your mind, that you may prove what is that good and acceptable and perfect will of God* (Rom. 12:1-2).

Paul again exhorts Timothy to yield to God's sanctifying work in his life. Speaking of God's power, Paul writes: *"Who has saved us and called us with a holy calling, not according to our works, but according to His own purpose and grace which was given to us in Christ Jesus before time began"* (2 Tim. 1:9). Although it would be Timothy's choice whether or not he would cooperate with God's work of sanctification, his ability to fulfill his ministry would directly depend upon how much he submitted to God's ongoing call of sanctification: *"Therefore if anyone cleanses himself from the latter, he will be a vessel for honor, sanctified and useful for the Master, prepared for every good work. Flee also youthful lusts; but pursue righteousness, faith, love, peace with those who call on the Lord out of a pure heart"* (2 Tim. 2:21-22).

A vessel is used to hold or to transport something – it is what a vessel does and not what it is that is important. Consequently, Scripture refers to individuals as vessels and states that God will use both the yielded and the rebellious vessels to work His eternal purposes and to uphold His glory. Timothy was implored by Paul to flee youthful lusts in order to be a vessel of honor fit for God's intended use. While on earth, only those Christians who yield to God's work of sanctification will practically experience the life of Christ in selfless service. "After sanctification," says Oswald Chambers, "it is difficult to state what your aim in life is because God has taken you up into His purposes."[1]

Submitting to God's ongoing call of sanctification enables one to know God's purpose for his or her life. Without the work of sanctification, service to God is impossible. Fanciful words and good intentions do not define a missionary, his or her character is the message and without Christ-likeness, he or she will fail miserably in representing Christ to the lost.

> Take time to be holy, speak oft with the Lord;
> Abide in Him always, and feed on His Word.
> Make friends of God's children; help those who are weak;
> Forgetting in nothing His blessing to seek.
> Take time to be holy, be calm in thy soul;
> Each thought and each motive beneath His control;
> Thus, led by His Spirit to fountains of love,
> Thou soon shall be fitted for service above.
>
> — William D. Longstaff

Service

The opportunity to please God through selfless service is made possible to those yielding to God's ongoing call of sanctification. As there is nothing in and of the flesh that can please God (Rom. 7:18), it is only those who continue to mortify the desires of the flesh and put aside their personal ambitions that are able to honor God through service.

The Lord Jesus gave individuals, such as evangelists and teachers, as gifts to the Church for a particular reason: *"for the equipping of the saints for the work of ministry, for the edifying of the body of Christ"* (Eph. 4:12). Every believer in the body of Christ has a work of ministry to engage in, the benefit of which will bless the entire body. As believers rightly use their spiritual gifts they equip others in the body to do ministry, which then passes the original blessing along to other believers in order to further edify the body. Visualize for a moment several children standing perfectly still in a wading pool while another child jumps into the pool. The resultant wave glides across the surface of the water and eventually bounces off every child in the pool. Each time the wave comes in contact with a child it is also reflected back across the pool, eventually making contact with every other child in the pool, and so on. This wave-motion phenomenon illustrates how the initial edification of one member in the body equips other members to minister to the body; the blessing then continues to spread throughout the body.

The outcome of such body-life enables individuals to reach their full potential in Christ and fulfill God's sovereign purpose for their lives. For example, though the evangelist is skillful in reaching the lost for Christ, his or her main ministry to the Church is to equip and to stir up others within the Body to evangelize wherever God has placed them as a testimony to the lost. The result of which is that, in a collective sense, the Church is stimulated and equipped to obey the great commission (Matt. 28:19-20).

Beneficial Church body-life is enjoyed as each member learns and practices sound doctrine while also learning how to properly use his or her spiritual gifts. Paul puts it this way: *"All Scripture is given by inspiration of God, and is profitable for doctrine, for reproof, for correction, for instruction in righteousness, that the man of God may be complete, thoroughly equipped for every good work"* (2 Tim. 3:16-17). Scripture supplies a foundation of truth for each believer to live out and practical sanctification occurs when he or she yields to It. Inevitably, all believers will suffer failure; conviction, correction, and reproof are God's means for restoring the wayward back to the path of righteousness. The Holy Spirit and other believers will be involved in this ministry, as well as providing further *training in righteousness* to enable the believer who stumbled to walk more successfully in the future. With spiritual maturity the prospect of God-honoring service becomes increasingly feasible.

Answer the Call

As already stated, this maturing process is enhanced by the practical equipping and correcting of others in the Body. Consider the following illustration as an example of this Body dynamic. Suppose a young man has a desire to be a carpenter, but has no practical experience. In preparation to become a carpenter he studies several textbooks on construction techniques, carpentry tools, and types of building equipment. He also reads a book entitled *Frequent Mistakes that Carpenters Make* to hopefully avoid future construction blunders. Is our self-motivated student a carpenter after he finishes these studies? Would you want him to build you a house? The answer to these questions is "No," he has no practical experience. However, after being mentored for a year by a veteran carpenter, the young man, who is still fervently studying his carpentry manuals, has become proficient in using carpentry tools, erecting walls, and even shingling a roof. Would you now be comfortable contracting the apprentice to construct your new home? No, he is growing in the trade and is a huge help to his mentor, but he still requires more training and learning opportunities. Though he will continue to learn about carpentry his entire life, in time, our diligent young man will obtain the necessary skill to erect a fine home and to train others to become carpenters also.

On the first day of training the veteran carpenter taught the apprentice *how* to properly drive a nail into wood – a fundamental skill in carpentry. Though the young apprentice had read about where to hit the nail with the hammer, how many blows would be required to drive different lengths of nails into various types of wood, and when to quit hammering to prevent wood damage, he actually had no practical experience in driving nails with a hammer. The master first showed the apprentice how to firmly hold the nail, saying, "If you hold the nail like this you won't smash your fingers and the nail won't eject from the wood when you hit it with a hammer." The master then demonstrated the proper technique for driving a nail by first setting the nail with a light tap of the hammer, and then by embedding the nail into the wood by a couple of smooth blows.

After these training exercises, the apprentice put into practice all that he had read, heard, and seen about driving nails. He smashed his finger once and bent several nails in the first few attempts, but as he continued to learn from his mistakes and the correction of the master he soon became proficient in driving nails. Nothing that the master taught contradicted the instruction of the carpentry manuals, yet his practical training and hands-on activities were necessary in the learning process. In the same way, the Word of God guides believers into all that is necessary to please the Lord, yet mentors are necessary to equip believers in the practical application of Scripture, and these believers must also exercise and develop their spiritual gifts in order to edify and bless the Church.

Paul's prayer for the believers at Colosse emphasizes this maturing process: *"that you may be filled with the knowledge of His will in all wisdom and spiritual understanding; that you may walk worthy of the Lord, fully pleasing Him, being fruitful in every good work and increasing in the knowledge of God"* (Col. 1:9-10). Note the progression from the knowledge of God, to the wisdom of that knowledge, to the outworking of both in fruitfulness, which then led to further knowledge of God. Not only were the believers to know the truth of Scripture, they were also to grow in wisdom (the practical outworking of understood truth).

This dynamic of practicing and experiencing the truth to learn wisdom was evident in the life of the Lord Jesus. Though He was full of truth (John 1:14), yet, He increased in wisdom and favor with God (Luke 2:52) and learned obedience by doing God's will for His life (Heb. 5:8). Experiencing the truthfulness of God's Word is necessary in the believer's life also. Tribulations, for example, practically test our faith and work into it a quality of patience that could not be achieved otherwise (Rom. 5:3; Jas. 1:3).

To be thoroughly equipped unto every good work, a believer, then, will rely on God's Word, the guidance of the Holy Spirit, and the mentoring assistance of spiritually-minded believers as he or she matures in Christ. Believers will accomplish their ministry within the body as they continue to grow spiritually, and exercise and develop their spiritual gifts. The world is not to be the believer's playground, its God's classroom. Believers are called to maturity and to service – the two cannot be separated. Scripture testifies to the fact that God grows ministries as He grows people.

For this reason Paul told Timothy, *"Do not neglect the gift that is in you, which was given to you by prophecy with the laying on of the hands of the eldership. Meditate on these things; give yourself entirely to them, that your progress may be evident to all"* (1 Tim. 4:14-16). Timothy had the advantage of apostolic authority publicly identifying his ministry, and it was not to be neglected. As he progressed in holiness and exercised his spiritual gift there would be greater ongoing benefit to the Church and also to Timothy personally. Later, Paul would exhort, *"I remind you to stir up the gift of God which is in you through the laying on of my hands. For God has not given us a spirit of fear, but of power and of love and of a sound mind"* (2 Tim. 1:6-7).

It is evident that Timothy answered the call to salvation, the call to sanctification, and the call to service. Paul told the church at Philippi that there was no other man as likeminded with him as Timothy; consequently, there was no question in Paul's mind that he would properly care for them when he arrived (Phil. 2:20). Timothy had learned that the greatest use of his life was to expend it for Christ; only then would he gain something that would outlast his own life and count for eternity. This understanding motivated Charles Spurgeon to write the following passionate letter to his son concerning the importance of missionary work:

> I should not like you, if meant by God to be a missionary, to die a millionaire. I should not like it, were you fitted to be a missionary, that you should drivel down to a king. What are all your kings, all your nobles, all your diadems, when you put them together, compared with the dignity of winning souls to Christ, with the special honor of building for Christ, not of

another man's foundation, but preaching Christ's Gospel in regions far behind.[2]

A Call to Promotion

Answering God's call results in promotion. By answering His call to salvation, an individual becomes a child of God and joint-heir with Christ. Responding to the ongoing call of sanctification improves one's moral wherewithal to be Christ-like. The process of sanctification also sharpens the believer's conscience in matters of right and wrong. Sanctification deflates our pride, self-illumination and personal ambitions. Answering the call of sanctification prepares one for service. To engage in service without sanctification would result in failure and ultimately bring reproach on the name of Christ. At the judgment seat of Christ each believer will receive a reward for all service that was done for Christ in God's strength and with proper motives. A. W. Tozer summarizes the matter this way:

> Before the judgment seat of Christ my service will not be judged by how much I have done but by how much of me there is in it. No man gives at all until he has given all. No man gives anything acceptable to God until he has first given himself in love and sacrifice.[3]

The paramount problem within the modern Church is that it is preoccupied with methods, traditions, and entertainment instead of with Christ, His Word, and His calling. Methods and traditions may have their place, but they should not replace the scriptural order, pattern, and purpose of the Church. The Church is an outpost of heaven on earth; it was never to be an amusement outlet with sensational attractions or a solemn sanctuary for pew-warmers. The Sovereign God of the universe is not fooled by either religious busyness or superficial stunts.

Individuals who ignore God's call to salvation in Jesus Christ can do nothing to please God (Rom. 10:1-3; Titus 1:16). Those ignoring God's call to sanctification in Jesus Christ also can do nothing to please God (Rom. 7:8, 8:8, 13). Finally, those ignoring God's call to service are pursuing their own agenda and, therefore, cannot please God (Eph. 2:10; 1 Pet. 1:10). God's callings are promotion offers that always better the individuals who answer. Those who choose to respond will glorify the Lord as they practically experience Him in their lives. So, dearly beloved of the Lord, answer God's call for your life – you will never regret it!

Name Calling

A few hours before His crucifixion, the Lord Jesus addressed His Father in prayer, *"I have manifested Your name to the men whom You have given Me out of the world"* (John 17:6). What did the Lord mean by the phrase, *"I have manifested Your name?"* He was acknowledging the fact that He had perfectly shown the nature of God to those He had been sent to declare God's message to. The Lord Jesus could only do what He saw His Father do (John 5:19) and that which would please His Father (John 8:29). The Lord could only speak His Father's words (John 12:48) and only do His will (John 5:30). Because the nature of God had been declared in every word and deed of the Lord Jesus, the name of God had wonderfully been displayed to the lost sheep of Israel.

The Lord Jesus considered the accurate manifestation of His Father's name to be a critical aspect of His ministry; He would do nothing to bring disdain or disgrace upon it. This is the example that the believer is to follow. The Bible refers to believers by various names, but two of these, "Christian" and "Church," specifically relate the *identity* of all believers in Christ to their *calling* in Christ.

"Christian"

Unfortunately, this term has come to mean something quite different from its original meaning found in Scripture. Today, many think that they are Christians because they have Christian parents or grandparents, or because they went to a church once in their life, or because they were baptized as a baby, or because they know something about Christ. The Lord Jesus makes it clear that it is not by knowing about Him that one becomes a Christian, but rather by knowing Him personally as Lord and Saviour (Matt. 7:21-23).

We read in Acts 11:26 that *"the disciples were first called Christians in Antioch."* "Christian" simply means "Christ-one" and refers to those who have trusted Christ alone for salvation. The word "disciple" is derived from the Greek word *mathetes*, meaning "a learner." What is a disciple to learn? The Lord Jesus answers this question:

> *Come unto me, all ye that labor and are heavy laden, and I will give you rest. Take my yoke upon you, and **learn of me**; for I am meek and lowly in heart: and ye shall find rest unto your souls. For my yoke is easy, and my burden is light* (Matt. 11:28-30, KJV).

The disciple of Christ is to learn Him. This is the only passage in the New Testament where the Lord personally informs His disciples of what He is like and tells them that they should learn of Him. The believer learns of the Lord's gentle and humble spirit when yoked with Him and he or she enjoys the peace of His presence in service when he or she rests in Him. The goal of discipleship emphasizes again that the Holy Spirit's work of sanctification is critical in a believer's life to effectively serve the Lord. To learn and to know Christ are integral to the sanctification process.

Consequently, doing important tasks in the name of Christ without bringing honor to His name is hypocrisy, not biblical discipleship. Profitable service to the Lord occurs as we learn Him. Not only does the believer learn Christ by spending time in His Word, but the believer is also increasingly transformed into Christ-likeness by the same activity (2 Cor. 3:18).

And is it so – I shall be like Thy Son?
Is this the grace which He for me has won?
Father of glory, thought beyond all thought!
In glory, to His own blest likeness brought!

— J. N. Darby

To completely identify with Christ, to learn of Christ (Matt. 11:29), and to be like Christ (Matt. 10:25) is the essence of biblical discipleship. This enables the called to know what the One calling is like. The extent to which this identification occurs will directly reflect how well the believer manifests the nature of Christ to the world.

Consider the following cases:

1. The Lord Jesus said to His disciples, *"By this all will know that you are My disciples, if you have love for one another"* (John 13:35). How would the world see Christ? When the disciples exhibited the same love for each other that Christ had already demonstrated to them.

2. Later the same evening, the Lord said to His Father, *"And the glory which You gave Me I have given them, that they may be one just as We are one: I in them, and You in Me; that they may be made perfect in one, and that the world may know that You have sent Me, and have loved them as You have loved Me"* (John 17:22-23). When would the glory of God's unity be manifested to the world? When the disciples were in a spirit of unity also.

3. Years later, Peter wrote to a persecuted group of Christians, *"Yet if anyone suffers as a Christian, let him not be ashamed, but let him glorify God in this matter"* (1 Pet. 4:16). Why could Peter encourage persecuted believers to suffer patiently for the cause of Christ? Because it would bestow glory to the name of God and mimic the example Jesus Christ lived out before men: *"But when you do good and suffer, if you take it patiently, this is commendable*

before God. For to this you were called, because Christ also suffered for us, leaving us an example, that you should follow His steps" (1 Pet. 2:20-21).

One by one, the disciples followed Christ's example; they answered God's call and suffered patiently for well-doing. Each faced death with the full assurance of God's Word; consequently hope, joy, and grace were enjoyed in the midst of tremendous testing. For example, history records that Aegeas crucified Andrew, Peter's brother, for his faith in Christ. Seeing his cross before him, Andrew bravely spoke, "O cross, most welcome and longed for! With a willing mind, joyfully and desirously, I come to thee, being the scholar of Him which did hang on thee: because I have always been thy lover, and have coveted to embrace thee."[1] Why could Andrew approach his cross with joy? He had watched the Lord approach His cross in the same manner.

A Christian is an ambassador for Christ (2 Cor. 5:20). He or she is a heavenly representative of Him on earth (Phil. 3:20). As faithfully as Christ declared the name of His Father during His earthly sojourn, the Christian is now to reveal to the world the name of the Lord Jesus Christ. This was Paul's prayer for the young believers at Thessalonica: *"That the name of our Lord Jesus Christ may be glorified in you, and you in Him, according to the grace of our God and the Lord Jesus Christ"* (2 Thess. 1:12).

Paul instructs Timothy as to what is necessary for Christians to adequately display the name of Christ: *"Let everyone who names the name of Christ depart from iniquity"* (2 Tim 2:19). Children imitate famous musicians by lip-syncing their songs on the radio, but believers cannot pretend to be holy; their conduct will either honor a sin-hating Saviour or endorse a Saviour-hating system. To declare the name of Christ is a high honor, but to associate with His name is the highest call to honor Him. To be identified as "a Christian" is one and the same as acknowledging Christ's call to live as He did.

"Church"

"Church" is another self-identifying term connected with the call to live unto Christ. The Greek word for church is *ekklesia*, which combines the preposition *ek*, meaning "out of," with a form of the Greek word *kaleo*, which as discussed earlier means "to bid" or "to call forth." Literally, "Church" means "a calling out" or, by implication, a "called out company." The Church's name defines its very essence. As individuals come to Christ for salvation, they are added to the Church. Through the power of the Holy Spirit, the cross of Christ carves them out of a dying and condemned world and securely places them in Christ as a "called out company."

What is meant when referring to the "world?" The world has different forms: political, artistic, musical, religious, entertainment, business, etc. Biblically speaking, the "world" may refer to the world we live in (the physical planet), the world of things, the world of people, or the world system controlled by Satan. In the latter instance, the world represents a human society built up apart from God; it is human civilization with its base motives and desires, the outworking of mankind's depraved state.

Worldliness, then, is any sphere in which the Lord Jesus is excluded. Ponder for a moment how the world's standard of success is in direct opposition to what the Lord Jesus taught:

The world wants service, but Christ says humble yourself and serve others.

The world says save your life, but the Lord says lose your life to gain one worth living.

The world exclaims "live for the moment," but Christians are to live for eternity.

The world says live for self, but the Lord says die to self.

The world is into power, but the Lord uses weak things to confound the mighty.

The world permits greed to rule distribution, but Christians are to give according to need.

The world says acquire wealth, but God says don't seek to be rich.

The world uses money and power to rule, but Christians are to pray and to use Scripture in love.

The world says retaliate and get even, but the Lord says repay evil with good and be forgiving.

The world uses violence, but Christians are to turn the other cheek.

So why is it that the world stands in opposition to Jesus Christ and His message? Why does the world exclude Christ from conversational, educational, and professional realms, but it is permissible to speak about world religion? It is because Satan is behind the scene, controlling the various systems of the world, and he despises Christ and those who identify with Him. Paul properly identifies Satan as *"the god of this age"* (2 Cor. 4:4) and *"the prince of the power of the air"* (Eph. 2:2). The Lord Jesus said on three occasions that Satan is *"the prince of this world"* (John 12:31, 14:30, 16:11). The world is Satan's delegated domain, but he must function within the boundaries which God allows. God is holy and He cannot tempt anyone to sin (Jas. 1:13), but Satan is allowed to test man's resolve to trust and obey God.

Consequently, the believer's thinking is to align with Christ's because he or she has been called out of the vain philosophies, human traditions, and the moral corruption of the world (Col. 2:8). The believer does not want to be under Satan's control or agenda because these are in direction opposition to Christ. For this reason, you may hear Christians say, "We are in the world, but not of the world" (see John 17:11, 16). As part of the Church, a true Christian's allegiance is to the Lord Jesus and not to the world; he or she is part of a *called out company* that has its sole identity and life in the Lord Jesus Christ.

The Reality of Identifying with Christ

For a number of years, our family's station wagon has displayed a gospel verse via a car magnet located just above the license plate. Although the intent of this magnet is to share the salvation message with others while venturing through traffic, the text has a sanctifying effect on my driving. Because I am publicly identifying with Christ, I am much more aware of my need to consecrate my right foot and to show kindness to other drivers. Increased personal identification with Christ results in increased personal sanctification to His will.

To be a "Christ-one" and to be a part of Christ's "called out company" is a great privilege and a high honor. May every believer understand that their identity in Christ conveys the strictest charge to honor Him in word and in deed. If you are a Christian, why not surround yourself with several daily reminders of your eternal calling in Christ (e.g. wear clothing that displays scriptural messages and decorate the walls of your home with Scripture texts).

Everyone that comes in contact with you should become aware of your association with Christ. Your modesty, your humility, your speech, and your genuine concern for others should testify that you have an intimate relationship with Jesus Christ. The Pharisees, for example, understood by the bold and wise behavior of the disciples *"that they had been with Jesus"* (Acts. 4:13). Believers are called to bring Christ into every situation of life – not to do so is to deny His Lordship.

"Everyone who is called by My name, whom I have created for My glory; I have formed him, yes, I have made him" (Isa. 43:7).

Come Out!

The word "come" formed the first heeded gospel message recorded in Scripture. God commanded Noah and his family to *come* into the ark to avoid destruction and they readily obeyed. Once they were sealed in the ark by God and with God their deliverance from God's wrath over wickedness was secure, but that was not all that God was accomplishing by the great flood. Certainly, the deluge destroyed life upon the earth, but it also lifted the ark off the earth to symbolize the separation from the world that God's people were to have. Salvation from hell and deliverance from the wickedness of the world are not independent realities with God. When God calls a person *out of* something it is in order *to enter* something else.

God's salvation for man is a complete salvation from sin and thus guarantees a consecrated people to God. Consequently, He warns both Old Testament and New Testament saints: *"Be holy, for I am holy."* As an example, what does Scripture reveal about God's plan to deliver the Israelites from Egypt? At the burning bush God presented His four-stage plan to Moses to prepare the Israelites for entering the promise land:

> *"So I have come down to deliver them out of the hand of the Egyptians, and to bring them up from that land to a good and large land, to a land flowing with milk and honey, ... Come now, therefore, and I will send you to Pharaoh that you may bring My people, the children of Israel, out of Egypt."... "I will certainly be with you. And this shall be a sign to you that I have sent you: When you have brought the people out of Egypt, you shall serve God on this mountain"* (Ex. 3:8-12).

33

God desired to deliver the Israelites first from bondage and secondly from Egypt itself. In allegory, the Israelites' slavery signifies the terrible bondage of sin we are born into and Egypt reflects a world system apart from God. These two agencies have caused man's misery since the fall in Eden. Thirdly, God desired to bless His people, but this would be contingent upon their complete obedience to His command to come to God at Mt. Sinai. Lastly, at Sinai they would serve the Lord. Clearly, obedience to the calls of deliverance and sanctification would precede the opportunity to serve God and to be blessed by Him.

As discussed in the previous chapter the Greek word for Church is *ekklesia*, which means "called out ones." Like the Israelites of old, the Church is a company of believers who have been or will be called out of several things. Randy Amos highlights six things believers have been called out of in Scripture:

They are called *out of* the world's mindset and system (John 15:19).

They are called *out of* the perishing nations (Acts 15:14).

They are delivered *from* this present evil age (Gal. 1:4).

They are delivered *from* the power of Satan's darkness (Col. 1:13).

They will be physically delivered *out of* this world and into heaven (2 Cor. 5:8; Rev. 3:10).

They are commanded to come *out of* the Babylonian system (Rev. 18:4).[1]

Three of these *called out* realities relate to the believer's positional salvation in Christ (Acts 15:14; Gal. 1:4; Col. 1:13). Every individual who trusts the gospel message of Jesus Christ is saved from eternal condemnation, the blinding darkness of Satan's deception, and a God-denying and self-exalting world system. Another *called out* reality relates to the future event when the Lord will return to the air to snatch up His Church from the earth and into heaven (2 Cor. 5:8; Rev. 3:10). The remaining two *called out* realities have particular relevance to the believer's sanctification. Throughout the Bible, God's people have been called out of two God-opposing ideologies. The first is the *world's pleasure* – a system of secular thinking which values the passing moment over the eternal purposes of God; the second is the *world's religion* – a system of humanized doings which devalue Christ's death and exalts self-improvement and self-worth.

It is these two *called out* realities, which pertain to the world's pleasure and the world's religion that are the particular focus of this chapter. Wherever God's people gather to form a local assembly of believers there will be some in that group who will tend to rely on legalism as the means for touting greater spirituality (i.e. these are pursing the world's religion), while others will tend to settle in and become spiritually lethargic (i.e. these fall prey to the world's pleasure). As examples, the church at Corinth was negatively influenced by the world's pleasure while the churches in Galatia were adversely affected by the world's religion. Consequently, it requires divine wisdom and grace to live out Christ-honoring liberty which seeks the good of others and the glory of God.

> Sanctification is not a heavy yoke, but a joyful liberation.
>
> — Corrie Ten Boom

Called out of the World's Pleasure

As stated earlier, worldliness is any sphere from which the Lord Jesus is excluded. The Lord Jesus told His disciples the night before He was crucified, *"If the world hates you, you know that it hated Me before it hated you. If you were of the world, the world would love its own. Yet because you are not of the world, but I chose you out of the world, therefore the world hates you"* (John 15:18-19). James likens worldliness to the sin of spiritual adultery: *"Adulterers and adulteresses! Do you not know that*

35

friendship with the world is enmity with God? Whoever therefore wants to be a friend of the world makes himself an enemy of God" (Jas. 4:4). Worldliness is the love of passing things, and things have no eternal value, except in how they are used to please God. Worldliness opposes God, and God hates it.

The story of Hosea and Gomer conveys a vivid picture to us of how God is offended by the worldly indulgence of His people. Hosea was an honorable man, but his wife Gomer was lascivious and actually conceived children that were not Hosea's. In time, Gomer abandoned Hosea to pursue a fast-life with her various lovers. It wasn't long before Gomer found herself in a poor and desperate situation. Hosea demonstrated sacrificial love for Gomer and sent supplies to her. With Hosea looking on from a distance, his wife Gomer praised her lovers for the very provisions he had sent to assist her (Hosea 2:5-8). Later, Gomer was abandoned by her lovers and sold into slavery. The redeeming love of God is exemplified when Hosea bought his own adulterous wife during a public slave auction. After experiencing the magnitude of Hosea's love, she would never depart from him or play the harlot again.

Paul reminds believers that they are the espoused bride of the Lord Jesus (Eph. 5:22-25; 2 Cor. 11:2; Rev. 19:9). If believers could understand Christ's redeeming love in even a small measure they would not commit adultery by fraternizing with the world. Why? Because it breaks the heart of Christ. The ideologies of the world oppose God and God opposes them. Gomer's lovers didn't care for Gomer or about the hurt they were causing Hosea; they used and abused Gomer until the thrill of the moment was gone. This was what the prodigal son learned in Luke 15; the world does not give anything that has lasting value, it only takes what is valuable to God.

Paul applies similar imagery in the New Testament by telling believers not to leave the Lord's Table to feast at the table of demons (1 Cor. 10:16-22). There is a spiritual table where the Lord resides with His people. At this table, full fellowship with God is enjoyed and all provision is made available for the believer to

36

spiritually thrive in life. All believers are seated at this table after trusting the gospel message and being born again. Why would anyone ever want to leave this table to party with demons?

These are vivid allegories to convey to us the heartbreak God suffers when His people desert Him and venture into the world to indulge their flesh and to dance with the devil. Paul warns, *"Do we provoke the Lord to jealousy? Are we stronger than He?"* (1 Cor. 10:22). Believer, are you provoking the Lord to jealousy by flirting with the world? If so, tell the Lord you are sorry and repent – or are you stronger than God? The Lord has no desire to destroy a rebellious child of His, but He has promised to chasten those He loves (Heb. 12:6). The choice is ours – to be hurt or to be helped by the Lord.

Worldliness is a system of thinking which is in direct opposition to the teachings of Christ. Erwin Lutzer puts the matter this way, "Worldliness is excluding God from our lives and, therefore, consciously or unconsciously accepting the values of a man-centered society," and "Worldliness is not only doing what is forbidden but also wishing it were possible to do it. One of its distinctives is mental slavery to illegitimate pleasure. Worldliness twists values by rearranging their price tags."[2] Often our flesh will try to justify the price tag of sin or questionable behavior, while our inner man is sounding the Philippians 4:8 alarm to exhort us to pursue the best and God-honoring course of action.

On a few occasions, I have enjoyed watching some wholesome science fiction movies, though these are becoming harder to come by. We do not watch TV in our home, but occasionally we do check out an old movie or documentary from the Library to watch together. Recently, my wife checked out a more modern and unrated Sci-Fi title for my personal enjoyment (she doesn't care for such things). Although the special effects were excellent, the plot was captivating, and the acting was outstanding, I noticed that I was fast forwarding through a number of unacceptable portions (romantic scenes, graphic violence, and new age propaganda). I returned the DVDs to my wife without viewing all of the media and asked her not to check them out again, saying, "I don't feel this is profitable for me to watch; the content is not all Christ-honoring." She said, "I appreciate your discernment; the cover looked questionable to me, so I had my doubts about the content." In one sense, it was a difficult thing to do, for the flesh definitely wants its way; however, the mental anguish of my conscience over the matter would far outlast the short-term thrill of Sci-Fi action – the price tag was too high.

In determining the appropriate response to questionable matters such as this, I have found it helpful to ask myself a few scripturally-based questions such as:

Do I have perfect faith that this activity is OK to do (Rom. 14:22-23)?

Could this activity master me (1 Cor. 6:12)?

Will this activity promote my own spiritual growth (1 Cor. 10:23)?

Will this activity bring glory to God (1 Cor. 10:31)?

Can I pray with a clear conscience that God will bless me in this activity (Phil. 4:6; 1 Thess. 5:17)?

Could this activity stumble a weaker brother in the Lord (1 Cor. 8:9)?

Will this activity unrighteously cause a lack of peace (Rom. 14:19a)?

Will this activity promote the spiritual growth of other believers (Rom. 14:19b)?

Could this activity hinder an unbeliever from receiving the gospel (1 Cor. 9:12, 10:33)?

By using Scripture to determine an appropriate response, the believer brings Christ's thinking into the situation in lieu of the world's wisdom. This is the means in which the *gray areas* of life are to be decided. Paul exhorts believers to *"work out* (not work for) *your own salvation with fear and trembling"* (Phil. 2:12).

This is a clear reference to sanctification, the process of God which delivers us from the *power* of sin. Trusting Christ for salvation delivers the believer from the *penalty* of sin through positional justification and the act of regeneration. In a future day, the believer will be delivered by resurrection power from the *presence* of sin into Christ's company forever (1 Thess. 4:13-18).

> Sanctification is not something our Lord does in me; sanctification is Himself in me.
>
> — Oswald Chambers

Resurrection power is something that each Christian can draw upon everyday in order to live out Christ's life (Phil 3:10). Paul wrote, *"I have been crucified with Christ; it is no longer I who live, but Christ lives in me; and the life which I now live in the flesh I live by faith in the Son of God, who loved me and gave Himself for me"* (Gal. 2:20). One cannot live Christ and still be enjoying the world's pleasure. Believer, measure your spirituality by your sensitivity to sin and your abhorrence of worldliness.

> There is nothing in common between the life of heaven and that of the world. It is not a question of prohibition as to using this or that, but of having altogether different tastes, desires, and joys. It is on this account that people imagine Christians are sad, for we do not enjoy the same things: The world does not know our joys; no unrenewed person can comprehend what renders a Christian happy.
>
> — J. N. Darby

Called out of the World's Religion

Perhaps you have heard someone say, "I have my own religion." Biblically speaking, this is a true statement; he or she is living out self-derived religion. The New Testament speaks of religion (*threskeia*) only four times and of traditionalized Judaism (*Ioudaismos*) only twice. Five of these six references to "religion" convey a negative sense of a humanized belief-system apart from God's truth – it is "man's religion." In the sixth reference, James speaks of *"pure religion"* as an outward behavior that perfectly practices what an individual believes to be true, without referring to a particular belief-system. Individuals who do not *practice* what they *preach* have a religion that is vain from a practical standpoint.

God is not impressed by religious rituals, developed church traditions, sanctimonious forms, and denominational smugness, but rather, delights in a personal lifestyle that conforms to divine truth (Col. 2:20-23). Christianity, therefore, is not a religion; however, when Christian doctrine is lived out it produces the right kind of religion, the kind that pleases God (Jas. 1:27). When one comes into a right relationship with God through the Lord Jesus Christ, then, and only then, is he or she able to please God by doing sincere and God-enabled deeds. World religion is an exhaustive system of *doings* apart from God's truth and God's assistance. It is dead religion and God calls His people "out of" its influence.

The intensity of this call is agonizingly apparent; God, speaking from heaven, is pleading with His people still on the earth to be holy people and to *come out* of the Babylonian religious system: *"And I heard another voice from heaven, saying,* **Come out of her, my people, that ye be not partakers of her sins,** *and that ye receive not of her plagues"* (Rev. 18:4). The mystery Babylon in the book of Revelation represents the culmination of world religion, a system of humanism that opposes God's message of truth and grace through Jesus Christ. Every aspect of this religious system is wicked and opposes God – no believer should have anything to do with it, now or in the future.

How did this system begin and how does it influence God's people today? First, let us consider the origin of world religion. The tenth chapter of Genesis identifies Babylon as the fountainhead of all pagan worship. The human founder of this system was Nimrod, whose name means "rebel." Even first century Jewish Historian Josephus regarded Nimrod as the father of pagan Babylonian and Assyrian cultures. Genesis 10:10 records that the Babylonians called their rising kingdom *Babel*, in their own estimation they were "the gate of God." They believed they could obtain divinity and be gods through human achievement.

Nimrod's quest for divinity would hinge on his success in constructing an enormous tower to bridge earth and heaven and close the gap between man and God. Obviously, such a tower was an affront against God, who is holy and separated from sinful man. Any attempt to bridge the distance between a Holy God and fallen mankind must be righteous in nature and God-ordained. Only the cross of Christ can bridge the gap between fallen humanity and holy deity.

Babylonian history records that Nimrod met with a sudden and violent death. His beautiful wife Semiramis, who had ascended by marriage from the common class to royalty, gave birth to what was said to be the essence of Nimrod (this was supposedly accomplished through soul transference). Her son Bacchus, which means "the lamented one," was said to be her deified husband.[3] Classical history refers to him as Nimus, meaning "the son," while Scripture calls him Tammuz in Ezekiel 8:14.[4]

Semiramis was licentious and gave birth to several children, though her husband was dead.[5] Her self-concocted story surrounding Nimus' birth not only secured her rule, but in time the people would reverence her as *Rhea*, "the great goddess mother,"[6] or *Beltis*, "the queen of heaven." She derived all her glory and her claim to deification through the very son she held in her arms. Ancient art depicting the mother and her son pose the glow of the sun behind each of their heads, indicating sun-divinity, but the glory of Semiramis was accentuated above that of her son.[7]

Given this brief history of the roots of paganism, let us investigate how respectable religions (apart from God's revelation) have evolved. The Chaldean version of Nimrod's story is that he prayed to the supreme God of heaven to take away his life, that his prayer was heard, and that he expired, assuring his followers that if they cherished due regard for his memory the empire would never depart from the Babylonians.[8] Because of his sacrifice he was allowed to come back again as his wife's son and have an improved position in life.

This idea of improving one's spiritual status or essence through subsequent lives has evolved into the teachings of reincarnation touted by many Eastern Religions and, more recently, by the New Age Movement. Today New Age propaganda has permeated the corporate, the educational, and the health care systems of the western world. It solicits followers into a self-help and self-improvement religion that undermines the vital need of a Saviour and the necessity of God's assistance in life.

Unfortunately, many professing Christians have been influenced by numerous New Age cults, sects, training seminars, television programs, healing techniques, etc. Some Christians have gone so far as to camouflage New Age mind imagery and visualization techniques into erroneous teaching on prayer: they say that positive faith constrains God's hand to bless you and negative faith allows Satan to move against you, so learn to pray with positive faith (i.e. positive thinking) so you can control God to bring about your visualized reality.

At the time of Nimrod, humanity had rebelled against God's command to spread out and populate the earth. Instead, most of them dwelt at Shinar and were engaged in constructing a huge tower, representing their human effort to become divine. The Lord stopped the work on the tower and spread mankind through the region by confounding their speech (Gen. 11:7-8). When the people dispersed, they also carried their developed pagan traditions with them. Consequently, the death (sacrifice) of the father god and the mother goddess and son story is found in many ancient cultures, but under different names. In Egypt, it is said that the miraculous birth of fair *Horus* resulted between the union of black *Osiris* who died and the mother goddess *Isis*.[9] The Assyrians wept for Tammuz, while in Greece and Rome the women wept for Bacchus when each sacrificially died for a better afterlife. Today, this repackaged pagan myth can be still witnessed in the teachings of the Roman Catholic Church, which refers to Mary as "the Queen of Heaven" and the "Mother of God." Many have ascribed glory to Mary in the same way Semiramis obtained deification – through the glory of her son.

This brief history highlights the rudiments of paganism and humanism which were incorporated into the Roman religious system. Unfortunately, many of these teachings have infiltrated and perverted much of the professing church for centuries. For example, many religious festivals were created to bridge heathen rituals with Roman Catholic celebrations in the fourth century (e.g. Christmas, Easter, and All Saints Day which is connected with Halloween); these and other religious practices resulted in a strong influx of wickedness into the Church. Goddess Mary has supplanted Christ's role as the sole mediator between God and men (1 Tim 2:5). Church tradition has superseded Scripture as God's sole expression of written Truth. The result is an elaborate system of humanized doings which has replaced Christ's propitiatory sacrifice as the sole means of reconciliation with God. The professing Church has been, and still is, adversely influenced by this world religious system.

World religion has always utilized self-contrived works to affirm human spirituality. Consequently, humanized Christianity has replaced the clear teachings of Scripture by promoting religious rituals and Church traditions as a means to measure one's religious status. We are creatures that want visible and audible confirmations of unseen spiritual realities, so we tend to create these to make ourselves feel secure. However, spirituality is not validated by the temporal manifestations of the flesh, but rather by the lack of them. A spiritual person, with the help of the Holy Spirit, lives out truth, not religious rote. Paul rebukes the legalists of his day for pushing their religious agenda on young Christians in Galatia in order to make a fair show of the flesh:

As many as desire to make a good showing in the flesh, these would compel you to be circumcised, only that they may not suffer persecution for the cross of Christ. For not even those who are circumcised keep the law, but they desire to have you circumcised that they may boast in your flesh. But God forbid

43

that I should boast except in the cross of our Lord Jesus Christ, by whom the world has been crucified to me, and I to the world (Gal. 6:12-15).

Legalism is a self-reckoned religious system of *doing* to improve one's spirituality or spiritual position. Though it began at Babel, it has confronted God's people since that time and is still an easy trap to fall into. In Paul's day, for example, the churches in Galatia were being told by Judaizers that though they were saved by grace through Christ, they had to keep the Law in order to maintain their salvation. This teaching meant that these Christians would lose their salvation as soon as they broke the Law, which was inevitable. By human reckoning, if doing something bad causes one to lose salvation, then something good must be done to convince one's self that salvation has been obtained again. Such teaching relies on works for salvation; God's grace and the assurance of eternal security that the Scripture offers is supplanted by a fear-based and flesh-exalting religious system.

Humanly speaking, we like some verification of where we are; we appreciate some kind of confirmation that we are on the right track and progressing along it. *Legalism,* however, will never be God's measurement stick for spirituality because it affronts His way of salvation and sanctification, which is by grace alone. Practically speaking, here are a few questions to ask yourself to see if you are following the heresy of legalism (i.e. measuring your spirituality by a fair show of your flesh).

Am I preoccupied with methods instead of Scriptural guidelines, principles, warnings, and commands?

Am I majoring on one truth to the exclusion of others?

Am I using one truth to compromise or to replace another truth?

Am I more concerned with theological nit-picking than with weightier matters of doctrine?

Am I offended by those who disagree with me in matters of preference and do I limit fellowship with them?

Am I spiritualizing or twisting Scripture in order to justify my theological position or church practice?

Am I emphasizing early Church patterns and practices more than specific Church truth revealed in the Epistles (e.g. speaking in tongues, frequency of the Lord's Supper)?

Am I relying on biblical parables and allegories for the basis for my doctrinal positions?

Am I more concerned with my outward appearance and how others perceive me than with how my inner man is developing and what the Lord thinks of me?

Am I promoting unity and growth in the body of Christ or causing disunity and hindering others from pursuing Christ?

Summary

Satan has been effective in deceiving humans into self-elevating religions and self-seeking practices. Through spiritual blindness (2 Cor. 4:3-4), Satan is able to convince man that his deep spiritual void can be satisfied with flesh-thrilling gimmicks or religious facades. The former numbs the conscience and the latter effectively locks the participant into a fear-based, work-based belief system. Both the world's pleasure and world's religion have the same end goal: to stimulate man's flesh to further sin against God, to be high on self, and to vent rage towards God. Without Christ, man has absolutely no hope of salvation and no hope of pleasing God.

Speaking of Christ, Peter proclaimed to the Sanhedrin (the Jewish judicial body): *"Nor is there salvation in any other, for there is no other name under heaven given among men by which we must be saved"* (Acts 4:12). They didn't like the Christian message and prohibited the apostles from speaking or teaching in the name of Jesus Christ (Acts. 4:18). Because the message of

Christ confronts the sinner to look honestly at his or her condition and to take sides with God against himself or herself, the name of Jesus Christ will always be inflammatory to those who reject His message. The power of Jesus' name to invoke both radical hatred within the rejecter (Luke 10:22) and immense love in the heart of a believer (1 Jn. 4:15-21) speaks of the supernatural power that His name carries. Consequently, when an individual calls upon the name of Christ for salvation, it is also true that Christ is calling him or her out of all that is ungodly and opposes His authority.

God is not merely concerned with saving lost souls, He also wants those who respond to His salvation call to be made completely conformable to the character of His Son (Rom. 8:29). Though believers will not obtain sinless perfection until they experience glorification (1 Cor. 15:51-52), the present desire of every believer should be to be like Christ, who is sinless (1 Pet. 2:22). Through Christ's blood the believer has the provision to be cleansed of sin and to be restored into happy fellowship with God (1 Jn. 1:9), but God's desire for us is that we do not sin at all (1 Jn. 2:1, 3:9).

Christ hates worldliness and so should His followers (Jas. 4:4). Accordingly, what the world runs after the Church should flee from. The Bible says, *"Abhor that which is evil; cleave to that which is good"* (Rom. 12:9) and *"Abstain from all appearance of evil"* (1 Thess. 5:22). The believer's attitude should not ask "how much worldliness can I get away with?" but rather, "how can I demonstrate love for the Lord Jesus by obeying His revealed Word?" (John 14:15). A believer can pursue spiritual sanctification only by devaluating the world's ideologies and religion, and then submitting to God.

"Are we prepared for what sanctification will do?" Oswald Chambers asks, "It will cost an intense narrowing of all our interests on earth and an immense broadening of our interest in God."[10] This is Paul's message to the Church at Colosse; may every child of God heed its exhortation:

If ye then be risen with Christ, seek those things which are above, where Christ sitteth on the right hand of God. Set your affection on things above, not on things on the earth. For ye are dead, and your life is hid with Christ in God. When Christ, who is our life, shall appear, then shall ye also appear with him in glory (Col. 3:1-4).

A dead body has no personal ambitions, no thought of enjoying the world's pleasure, no wherewithal to make a fair show of its flesh. A corpse is not offended by the world's insults nor is it able to strike back when attacked. A corpse has no rights. Positionally speaking, all believers died with Christ some 2000 years ago (Rom. 6:1-10); thus, we have no personal rights anymore to live the way we naturally would apart from Christ.

Die before you die. There is no chance after.

— C. S. Lewis

There was a day I died, utterly died, died to George Muller, His opinions, preferences, tastes, and will – died to the world, its approval or blame – even of my brethren and friends since then I have studied only to show my self approved unto God.

— George Muller

As a direct result of being declared dead in Christ, believers, in the positional sense, have also been made alive with Him. This spiritual reality ensures that we have *"all spiritual blessing in heavenly places"* at our disposal to live a life that is pleasing to the Lord (Eph. 1:3). So live out Christ's life, dear believer, and avoid the crippling influences of the world's pleasure and the world's religion.

In every Christian's heart there is a cross and a throne, and the Christian is on the throne till he puts himself on the cross; if he refuses the cross, he remains on the throne. Perhaps this is at the

bottom of the backsliding and worldliness among gospel believers today. We want to be saved, but we insist that Christ do
all the dying. No cross for us, no dethronement, no dying. We
remain king within the little kingdom of Mansoul and wear our
tinsel crown with all the pride of a Caesar; but we doom ourselves to shadows and weakness and spiritual sterility.[11]

— A. W. Tozer

Doing the Will of God

"I want to know the will of God for my life," a young person exclaimed. I replied, "Good, do you know what God's will for your life is as it is revealed in Scripture?" The resulting perplexed expression answered my question. I continued, "Before you can possibly know God's purpose for your life you must be following His will in your life; Paul instructs believers to *'be not unwise, but understanding what the will of the Lord is'"* (Eph. 5:17). The will of God, as revealed in Scripture, is the same for all believers. This is where each Christian must initiate his or her quest to please God.

Normally, when Scripture speaks of "the will of God," it explicitly states what it is; there is no mystery about it, God has declared to us His will for our lives. As we learn to align our will with God's general will for us, we become more able to sense His specific calling. God grows people as He grows ministries, otherwise the ministry would be a disaster rather than a good testimony of Christ.

Ministry requires the preparatory work of building godly character, faith, and tenacity into an individual. Moses had forty years in Egypt and forty years on the backside of a desert before he was prepared for the ministry. John the Baptist was thirty years old before he became the *"voice of one crying in the wilderness."* Paul was saved approximately ten years before he was called into action, and a portion of that time was spent being taught by the Holy Spirit in the Arabian Desert. Before we can profitably engage in service, we must be broken to the will of

God; otherwise, we are just disguising personal agendas as spiritual ministries.

> We need to remember that we cannot train ourselves to be Christians; … we cannot bend ourselves to the will of God: we have to be broken to the will of God.[1]
>
> — Oswald Chambers

> To accept the will of God never leads to the miserable feeling that it is useless to strive anymore. God does not ask for the dull, weak, sleepy acquiescence of indolence. He asks for something vivid and strong. He asks us to cooperate with him, actively willing what he wills, our only aim his glory.
>
> — Amy Carmichael

The first step to brokenness is to know what the will of God is. That is, it is to understand what God's general will is for one's life. Here is a summary; each of the referenced passages below is directly tied to the phrase "the will of God" and is explained in the following pages:

1. Serve and please the Lord instead of men (Eph. 6:6).

2. Do not be conformed to the world (Rom. 12:2).

3. Put the ignorance of foolish men to silence by well-doing (1 Pet. 2:15).

4. Abstain from fornication (1 Thess. 4:3).

5. Give thanks in everything (1 Thess. 5:18).

6. Suffer for well-doing, rather than for evil-doing (1 Pet. 3:17).

7. Do not be controlled by the lusts of the flesh (1 Pet. 4:2).

Serve the Lord instead of Men

Proverbs 29:25 reads, *"The fear of man brings a snare, but whoever trusts in the Lord shall be safe."* The real driving force behind the *fear of man* is what the writer of Hebrews describes as the *"fear of death,"* although the writer then acknowledges that Christ has released *"those who through fear of death were all their lifetime subject to bondage"* (Heb. 2:15-16). The fear of men is rooted in the dread of personal harm. Why did the Pharisees fear arresting Jesus Christ? It was not because they thought He was the Son of God, but rather because they feared a revolt by the people, which might do them harm (Matt. 21:26, 46).

The Lord Jesus said that believers should not fear anyone or anything but God Himself (Matt. 10:28). As the believer learns to fear and respect only the Lord, his or her mind is liberated to serve God as he or she is motivated by love. Why? Because *"there is no fear in love; but perfect love casts out fear, because fear involves torment. But he who fears has not been made perfect in love"* (1 Jn. 4:18). The judgment of our sin is past; consequently believers are secure in Christ forever. In recognition of this, Christians are propelled to service not by a spirit of fear but out of love for the Lord; this gives their service value. World religion motivates its captives to serve out of fear, but this is not God's way.

It wasn't until Peter had settled the *death* question that he was made useful for the kingdom of God. He had forsaken all for the Lord (his occupation, his family, his home, etc.), but Peter learned on the night that the Lord was arrested that this was not enough to live for the Lord. It seems Peter was willing to die for the Lord at the Lord's arrest: Peter risked his life and wielded his sword against overwhelming numbers to protect the Lord. Peter didn't understand that the Lord needed no body guard to ensure His safety, for the arrest and the events that followed were completely in His control. The lesson Peter would learn that night was that it is harder to live for the Lord than it is to die for Him. Only a few hours later, Peter, because of the fear of men, would vehemently deny the Lord Jesus.

Until a believer settles the death question and resolves to die daily for Christ, he or she will find it difficult to live for Christ. A fearful believer will have a poor testimony for Christ. Peter learned this lesson the hard way, but after being restored to Christ, he preached a message in which 3,000 souls were won to Christ (Acts 2). How about you – are you willing to die daily to serve the Lord, or will you serve men because you fear them more than you reverence Christ? Joshua's appeal to the Lord's people 3,500 years ago is still valid today:

> *Now therefore, fear the Lord, serve Him in sincerity and in truth, and put away the gods which your fathers served.... But as for me and my house, we will serve the Lord* (Josh. 24:14-15).

Another wrong motivation for service, besides the fear of men, is the praise of men. If our ministry is motivated by the praise of men it has no value to God because we are promoting ourselves and not Him (Luke 18:10-14). Two men were once discussing how one can know when he or she has become a true servant of God. One man said, "You know you are a servant of God when others start treating you like a servant." The other man countered, "I think that you will know you are a servant of God by how you act when others treat you like a servant." To regard the good of others and not our own is the epitome of God-honoring service. A servant of God longs to serve, but does not promote himself – it is God alone who does the promoting.

Finally, we would do well to remember that it is not our personal achievements that result in satisfaction, but rather doing the will of God from a pure heart: *"Be obedient ... with fear and trembling, in sincerity of heart, as to Christ; not with eyeservice, as men-pleasers, but as bondservants of Christ, **doing the will of God from the heart,** with goodwill doing service, as to the Lord, and not to men"* (Eph. 6:6). A pure heart delights in doing the will of God regardless of what men think.

Do Not be Conformed to the World

This is a hard subject to speak about without sounding legalistic. As already mentioned in the previous chapter the clear *dos* and *don'ts* of God's Word frame the Christian's conduct. The warnings, guidelines, examples of lessons-learned, and principles of Scripture are the instruments that are needed to complete the portrait of a godly life within this frame. The frame will be the same for everyone, but the artistic flare of the image (the individual testimony) it encloses will be different for each believer as each one works out the gray areas with fear and trembling before the Lord (Phil. 2:12). However, each portrait is to be a living testimony of Christ. The light of Christ must be seen and not hidden in the portrait.

The Lord Jesus instructed His disciples to let their testimony for Him shine brightly in a dark world:

> *You are the light of the world. A city that is set on a hill cannot be hidden. Nor do they light a lamp and put it under a basket, but on a lampstand, and it gives light to all who are in the house. Let your light so shine before men, that they may see your good works and glorify your Father in heaven* (Matt. 5:14-16).

Many years ago there was a terrible accident in which several youths were killed when their car was struck by a train. At the trial, the watchman was questioned: "Were you at the crossing the night of the accident?"

"Yes, your Honor."

"Were you waving your lantern to warn of the danger?"

"Yes, your Honor," the man told the judge.

But after the trial had ended, the watchman walked away mumbling to himself, "I'm glad they didn't ask me about the light in the lantern, because the light had gone out."[2]

When a believer conforms to the world the light of his or her testimony is smothered. Consequently, Christ will not be made known to the lost and souls that might have been reached with the gospel will perish. Does you life warn the lost of danger or has conformity extinguished your testimony for Christ?

Silence Fools by Well-doing

To a group of scattered Christians enduring tremendous persecution Peter wrote: *"For this is the will of God, that by doing good you may put to silence the ignorance of foolish men"* (1 Pet. 2:15). The Lord Jesus likewise instructed His disciples, *"But I say to you, love your enemies, bless those who curse you, do good to those who hate you, and pray for those who spitefully use you and persecute you"* (Matt. 5:44). Paul wrote to the Galatians, *"Therefore, as we have opportunity, let us do good to all"* (Gal 6:10), and to the Romans he exhorted:

> *Repay no one evil for evil. Have regard for good things in the sight of all men. If it is possible, as much as depends on you, live peaceably with all men. Beloved, do not avenge yourselves, but rather give place to wrath; for it is written, "Vengeance is Mine, I will repay," says the Lord.* (Rom. 12:17-19).

A few verses later Paul instructed the Christians in Rome to, *"Owe no one anything except to love one another, for he who loves another has fulfilled the law"* (Rom. 13:8). He had already told them that the purpose of the Law was to show man his sin and need for a Saviour (Rom. 3:20-25). If someone stole something, it proved that they could not *keep* the law and that they were sinful. The Law declares God's holiness and man's depravity. But once the Holy Spirit indwells a believer, he or she becomes able to *fulfill* the righteousness of the Law and in so doing displays the love of God. Consequently, those who have experienced the love of God will delight to fulfill His Law; they will long to express love back to Him through obedience. For example, he or she will have no desire to have other gods (Ex. 20:3), or to use God's name vainly (Ex. 20:7), love forbids such behavior.

How is this possible? Paul explains that it is Christ working in the believer through the Holy Spirit: *"That the righteous requirement of the law might be fulfilled in us who do not walk according to the flesh but according to the Spirit"* (Rom. 8:4). As a believer chooses not to hinder the Spirit's working (i.e. does not follow the desires of his or her flesh) the righteousness of the Law becomes evident in that individual's life; it is an outward expression of Christ's inward working. For example, when one chooses not to steal, he or she has kept the Law; however, fulfilling the Law is more than just not stealing from another – it is giving to that person. As sacrificial giving is an expression of divine love, in this instance of behavior, the Law has been fulfilled by the believer.

Indeed, God's holiness is reflected when a person *keeps the Law* (which no one can do, naturally speaking), but His gracious character is represented when one *fulfills the law*. Through the power of the Holy Spirit, the believer conveys the love of God to others in a supernatural way. It is not natural to love our enemies, to do good to those who persecute us, to bless those who curse us, or to withhold vengeance when it is just. Yet, this is what the believer is commanded to do because it is the will of God: *"He who does not love does not know God, for God is love"* (1 Jn. 4:8). God is the source of all true love.

God extended His love to mankind by the giving of His own Son as a substitutionary sacrifice (1 Jn. 4:9-10). The result, *"We love Him, because He first loved us"* (1 Jn. 4:19). As the *"Him"* in this verse is not found in the Greek text the meaning of the verse is simply this: His love causes our love. The same cause and effect phenomenon witnessed in physical creation is also observed in God's love. The *cause* is His love and the *effect* is our love. Accordingly, there can be no happiness in just receiving God's love; it must be passed along to experience joy. God's love was not sourced to us to be absorbed and hoarded, it is to be directed back to God in heart-felt appreciation and devotion or to be reflected to others that they might witness God's love in action and then direct praise back to God also.

So when people-problems are overwhelming you, choose to rejoice in the Lord, pray for help, and then resort to love when responding to the situation. The more you are hated, the more you should love. Usually, in God's time, the oppressor will break down because God's love is irresistible.

We once had an unsaved neighbor whose demeanor towards our family was unjustly harsh. Our family showed consistent kindness to our rude and caustic neighbor for seven years without a favorable response. However, on one frigid morning after a significant snowfall, our grumpy neighbor surprised us by arriving at our home with his tractor. Without saying a word he promptly cleared away the snow from our long driveway. Our family watched from the living room picture window in disbelief. I turned to the children and said, "See guys, love really does work." When he was finished, I ventured outdoors to thank him and to hand him a cup of coffee. I will never forget his words: "I just wanted to say thank you for being nice neighbors." God's love in action is a wonderful resource to bring even the vilest sinner to his knees!

Abstain from Fornication

There is absolutely no middle ground on this command: *"For this is the will of God, your sanctification: that you should abstain from sexual immorality"* (1 Thess. 4:3). Fornication is any sexual relationship outside the confines of matrimony. Premarital sex, adultery, homosexual unions, etc. are all outside the will of God – these sins pervert His order for mankind. Sexual immorality is a mark of a false teacher (2 Pet. 2:14) and a litmus test to indicate whether someone is truly saved. Paul says no one continuing in fornication will inherit the kingdom of God (Eph. 5:5). John emphatically states that those continuing in fornication will spend eternity in the lake of fire (Rev. 21:8).

Paul acknowledges that there were some in the Church at Corinth that had been fornicators before answering the call to salvation: *"And such were some of you. But you were washed, but you were sanctified, but you were justified in the name of the Lord Jesus and by the Spirit of our God"* (1 Cor. 6:11). The Greek verb translated "were" in the beginning of this verse is in the *imperfect* tense, meaning that some of the Corinthians were active fornicators until they trusted Christ, after which they ceased from immoral behavior. It is noted that the Greek verb translated "were washed" in this verse is in the aorist indicative middle voice, meaning that the Corinthians had made a personal choice in the past on their own behalf to be washed clean by the blood of Christ. This shows human responsibility to answer the call of salvation and God's response to positionally sanctify in Christ those who answer the call. Their choice of Christ for salvation resulted in their repudiation of fornication also. The world continues to degrade and mock God's plan for marriage and promote its own agenda for sexual pleasure. J. I. Packer summarizes God's purpose for the sexual union of a husband and wife:

> God intends, as the story of Eve's creation from Adam shows, that the "one flesh" experience should be an expression and a heightening of the partner's sense that, being given to each other, they now belong together, each needing the other for completion and wholeness. Children are born from their relationship, but this is secondary: what is basic is the enriching of their relationship itself through their repeated "knowing" of each other as persons who belong to each other exclusively and without reserve.[3]

A husband proves his manhood not by becoming one flesh with many women, but by sacrificially loving one woman, his wife, and romancing her for life. Fornication is not only a grievous sin against one's own body (1 Cor. 6:18), it degrades the value of marriage. A believer cannot engage in fornication without defiling the temple of God, his or her own body (1 Cor. 6:19). A defiled temple cannot be used to worship a Holy God anymore than a prostitute could be an honorable wife. Not only are believers not to engage in fornication, they are not to even joke about or make light of this grievous sin (Eph. 5:3-4) or delight in watching others engage in it (Rom. 1:32). As stated earlier, there is no middle ground on this matter; if you want to do the will of God, you must abstain from sexual immorality.

Give Thanks in Everything

Why does Paul tell the Thessalonians to *"In everything give thanks; for this is the will of God in Christ Jesus for you"* (1 Thess. 5:18)? Because *"we know that all things work together for good to them that love God, to them who are the called according to His purpose"* (Rom. 8:28). This means that, God has us right where He wants us in order to extend the most benefit and to effect His glory. Does a derogatory spirit strangle your mind from thinking positively? That is, do you see a half-empty glass of water or a half-full glass? The reality has not changed, but your perception of it has. Do the blooms of the rose bush or its thorns capture your attention? Thankful and belittling mind frames do not enjoy each other's company.

There is always something to be thankful for if one is in the right frame of mind to look for it. When the antique vase accidentally slips from your hands and shatters into a thousand pieces upon its impact with the floor, praise the Lord it did not hit your foot. If you are involved in a traffic accident in which your vehicle is ruled a total wreck, praise the Lord you were kept safe. After being robbed, Matthew Henry penned His thankfulness to God: "Let me be thankful, first, because he never robbed me before; second, because although he took my purse, he did not take my life; third, because although he took all I possessed, it was not much; and fourth, because it was I who was robbed, not I who robbed."[4] A thankful mind frame will always find something to praise God about, no matter how challenging the trial is.

Hudson Taylor devoted his life to being a missionary in China through the heart of the 19th century. His vision for evangelism established the China Inland Mission, which successfully solicited thousands of missionaries to venture to China while he coordinated their activities. Tens of thousands of souls were saved.

The years in China were difficult for Taylor, but the fruitfulness of his labor is evident to this day. The fiery trials brought fresh realization that he was just a vessel in the Lord's hands to be used as his Master saw fit. Diseases claimed the lives of two of the Taylors' children. Hudson and his wife Maria sent their remaining four children back to England with a trusted friend to be educated and kept safe. Shortly after this, Maria Taylor gave birth to a fifth son, but within a week, cholera took this child's life also. Soon after this, his beloved wife became very ill. Hudson came to the bed of his 33-year-old wife and said, "My darling, do you know that you are dying?" "Can it be so? I feel no pain, only weariness," was her reply. "Yes, you are going home. You will soon be with Jesus." Hudson said. His dying wife then apologized for leaving him alone in such difficult times.

Mrs. Duncan, an eyewitness of Mrs. Taylor's homegoing, later wrote of the event:

> I never witnessed such a scene. As dear Mrs. Taylor was breathing her last, Mr. Taylor knelt down – his heart so full – and committed her to the Lord; **thanking Him** for having given her and for the twelve and a half years of happiness they had had together; **thanking Him**, too, for taking her to His own blessed presence, and solemnly dedicating himself anew to His service.[5]

With three of his seven children dead, the other four in England, and now his beloved wife home with Lord, Hudson wrote:

> From my inmost soul I delight in the knowledge that God does or deliberately permits all things and causes all things to work together for good to those who love Him (Rom. 8:28). ... I saw that **it was good** for the Lord to take her, **good indeed for her**, and in His love He took her painlessly; and **not less good for me** who must henceforth toil and suffer alone – yet not alone,

for God is nearer to me than ever. And now I have to tell Him all my sorrows and difficulties, as I used to tell dear Maria.[6]

Shortly after this great trial of faith Hudson wrote to Mrs. Berger, "No language can express what He has been and is to me. Never does He leave me; constantly does He cheer me with His love."[7] Hudson focused his mind on the good that God was accomplishing through the trial and thus, he could be thankful. The result of that was a closer fellowship with the Saviour and a sanctified vessel for His use.

Thanksgiving and contentment are closely related. Paul informs the Christians at Philippi of what he had learned about contentment and thankfulness:

> *I have learned in whatever state I am, to be content: I know how to be abased, and I know how to abound. Everywhere and in all things I have learned both to be full and to be hungry, both to abound and to suffer need. I can do all things through Christ who strengthens me* (Phil. 4:11-13).

Paul instructed Timothy, *"Now godliness with contentment is great gain. For we brought nothing into this world, and it is certain we can carry nothing out. And having food and clothing, with these we shall be content"* (1 Tim. 6:6-8). Verse 10 of that chapter speaks of those who were discontent and unthankful for what God had provided. They coveted money and erred from the faith. If God wanted us to have more than what we have, He would have bestowed it upon us. Being thankful defeats dissatisfaction.

The root of sin seems to be dissatisfaction, with selfishness and pride trailing close behind. When we are not content with what we have, we murmur against God. Murmuring is half-uttered complaints that God hears anyway. It results from looking backwards instead of Godward. The nation of Israel grumbled and complained the whole time they were in the Sinai Peninsula. Why? Because they were always comparing

60

what they had at the moment to what they once had in Egypt–
in slavery!

> *And the whole congregation **of the children of Israel mur-mured against Moses and Aaron in the wilderness**: And the children of Israel said unto them, Would to God we had died by the hand of the Lord in the **land of Egypt**, when we sat by the flesh pots, and when we did eat bread to the full; for ye have brought us forth into this wilderness, to kill this whole assembly with hunger* (Ex. 16:2-3, KJV).

> *And the people thirsted there for water; **and the people murmured against Moses**, and said, Wherefore is this that thou hast brought us up out of **Egypt**, to kill us and our children and our cattle with thirst?* (Ex. 17:3, KJV).

We complain and grumble today because our expectations are not met in comparison to what we had the month before. Last month we complained because again our expectations were not satisfied when compared to the previous month. Looking backwards at what once was and comparing it to our wanton expectations leads to complaining. The spiritual response to all of our life's situations is to look for the good, to be thankful in all things, and to cease peering into history and comparing your situation with what was or what somebody else has.

> *Every good gift and every perfect gift is from above, and comes down from the Father of lights, with whom there is no variation or shadow of turning* (Jas. 1:17, KJV).

Suffer for Well-doing
Peter wrote the following to a group of persecuted believers:

> *For it is better, if it is the will of God, to suffer for doing good than for doing evil. For Christ also suffered once for sins, the just for the unjust, that He might bring us to God, being put to death in the flesh but made alive by the Spirit* (1 Pet. 3:17-18).

Napoleon Bonaparte once said, "It requires more courage to suffer than to die."[8] He also noted that, "It is the cause, and not the death, that makes the martyr."[9] After a heart-wrenching denial, Peter found the first statement to be true: he learned that it requires more courage to suffer daily for the Lord than to die once for Him. Ultimately, after finishing his course in life, Peter would die for the Lord. Though Peter was crucified upside-down (because he thought himself unworthy of being crucified the same way his Lord was) he understood that it was not the details of his death that were important, but rather the cause for which he had lived and for which he was ready to die for – the cause of Christ.

Simply put, it is easier to die for the Lord than it is to live for Him by daily dying to self. There is no room for self-will, self-ambition, or self-exaltation in a life lived for Christ, and all those who lose their life for Christ's sake *"shall suffer persecution"* (2 Tim. 3:12). To suffer patiently for God takes real courage! Nowhere in Scripture is this truth more evident than in the example of our Lord Jesus Christ at Calvary.

Matthew tells us that at the beginning of that day both thieves blasphemed the Lord (Matt. 27:44); however, Luke informs us that one thief had a change of heart. Sometime within those three morning hours this thief came to understand that he was a sinner, that he was rightly being punished for his crimes, and that Jesus Christ was the only means of saving his soul.

What sign, what message, what miracle caused this thief to be converted? It was the patient suffering of an innocent Saviour who never reviled His oppressors but rather demonstrated love for them through this intercession for them. The repentant thief knew that this was a supernatural feat, an authentic demonstration of divine grace at work. In the same way, as a believer suffers patiently for the Lord a sweet savor of Christ is provided to a lost world; it is a savor of life unto life for those who repent, but it is a savor of death unto death to those who perish (2 Cor. 2:14-16). The knowledge of Christ in the believer's life, therefore, is to be an unavoidable fragrance to the lost. This was Christ's testimony at Calvary and we should follow His example:

For what credit is it if, when you are beaten for your faults, you take it patiently? But when you do good and suffer, if you take it patiently, this is commendable before God. For to this you were called, because Christ also suffered for us, leaving us an example, that you should follow His steps: "Who committed no sin, nor was deceit found in His mouth;" who, when He was reviled, did not revile in return; when He suffered, He did not threaten, but committed Himself to Him who judges righteously; who Himself bore our sins in His own body on the tree, that we, having died to sins, might live for righteousness — by whose stripes you were healed (1 Pet. 2:20-24).

Suffering patiently for the cause of Christ is a token of perdition to the lost and a token of salvation to the believer (Phil. 1:28; 2 Thess. 1:5). As shown in the conversion of the repentant thief, suffering with patience while relying on God's grace is a supernatural testimony to the lost; it is nonetheless a consolation to the believer that he or she is truly a child of God. Praying for those who persecute you is a demonstration of God's control of your will and it will be a safeguard to your mind – a defense against bitterness and overwhelming sorrow.

History records the intense persecution of the Church by the Roman Empire, but what is not as well-documented is the impact that the patient suffering of the early Church had on specific leaders within the empire. When Pliny was governor of Bithynia (about A. D. 110), he wrote a letter to the Roman Emperor Trajan to ask why Christians were being exterminated, then added:

I have been trying to get all the information I could regarding them. I have even hired spies to profess to be Christians and become baptized in order that they might get into the Christian services without suspicion. Contrary to what I had supposed, I find that the Christians meet at dead of night or at early morn, that they sing a hymn to Christ as God, that they read from their own sacred writings and partake of a very simple meal consisting of bread and wine and water (the water added to the wine to dilute it in order that there might be enough for all). This is all that I can find out, except that they exhort each other to be subject to the government and to pray for all men.[10]

Pliny also informed Emperor Trajan how he rooted out the Christians in his area: "I gave these men chance to invoke the gods of Rome, offer sacrifice to the image of the Emperor, and finally to curse the name of Christ," but that "none of these acts, those who are really Christians can be forced to do."[11]

Not only is patiently suffering for the cause of Christ a testimony of supernatural wherewithal to the lost, but Paul told the saints at both Philippi and Thessalonica that it was a token (a proof) of their salvation. John Wesley rode tens of thousands of miles on horseback to carry the gospel message from town to town and house to house some 250 years ago in the United Kingdom. According to his journal he often preached two or three messages a day. He was often persecuted for his work; in fact, to Wesley the lack of persecution was a troubling sign of broken fellowship with God.

On one occasion, John Wesley was riding along a road when it dawned on him that three whole days had passed in which he had suffered no persecution. No brick or even an egg had been thrown at him for three days! Alarmed, he stopped his horse and exclaimed, "Can it be that I have sinned, and am backslidden?" Slipping from his horse, Wesley went down on his knees and began interceding with God to show him where, if any, there had been a fault. A rough fellow on the other side of the hedge, upon hearing the prayer, looked across and recognized the preacher. "I'll fix that Methodist preacher," he said, and then he proceeded to pick up a brick and hurl it at John Wesley. It missed its mark and fell harmlessly beside Wesley, whereupon he leaped to his feet joyfully exclaiming, "Thank God, it's all right. I still have His presence."[12]

May each believer live to please Christ, understanding that this will result in suffering, but also knowing that perseverance is pleasing to the Lord, strengthens our resolve to live for Christ, and is a testimony of the power of the gospel to the lost. Are you suffering for the cause of Christ? If so, are you doing so with patience?

Do Not be Controlled by Lusting

There are many areas in which our flesh can lust: for social status, for fame, for food, for vices, for sexual pleasures, for money, for beauty, etc. It is impossible to allow our flesh to continue to long for these things and not have our behavior adversely affected. Peter acknowledges that a believer cannot live in the flesh and be in the will of God at the same time (1 Pet. 4:2). Paul emphasizes the same truth when writing the Christians at Rome:

> For those who live according to the flesh set their minds on the things of the flesh, but those who live according to the Spirit, the things of the Spirit. For to be carnally minded is death, but to be spiritually minded is life and peace. Because the carnal mind is enmity against God; for it is not subject to the law of God, nor indeed can be. So then, those who are in the flesh cannot please God (Rom. 8:5-8).

As we have already learned, if we are going to do God's will we must abstain from fornication. If we are to abstain from fornication, we must put up a defense that will maintain our thought-life in purity. We cannot lust in our members and expect to be holy in conduct. The Lord Jesus said that if a man looks on a woman with lust he has already committed sexual immorality with her in his heart (Matt. 5:28).

Physically, we are what we eat; spiritually, we are what we think: *"For as he thinketh in his heart, so is he"* (Prov. 23:7). By properly controlling our thought-life we control our behavior! By choosing not to stimulate our flesh through suggestive media we find it easier to control our thought-life. Unchecked lust leads to sin and separation from God (Jas. 1:14); He cannot have fellowship with us while we are in sin (1 Jn. 1:5-7).

The mind is the battle zone for all one's conduct. Over time, the heart is shaped by what the mind repeatedly thinks about; moral decisions form a pure heart, while immoral choices strengthen its inherent depravity. A pure heart will freely exercise faith, demonstrate love, and rejoice in hope, but a depraved heart loves only sin. A person's thought-life follows the sowing and reaping principles of the harvest. The three laws of the harvest are: (1) you reap what you sow; (2) you reap more than what you sow; and (3) you reap later than you sow. Paul explains that if *"a man soweth to his flesh, he shall of the flesh reap corruption"* (see Gal. 6:7-8). Others may not know of your secret sins, but God knows and you know, so *"be sure your sin will find you out"* (Num. 32:23).

When a believer feeds on (thinks upon) what is corrupt, it leads to a legitimate harvest of corruption. He or she will realize, long after the initial seeds were sown, that the repercussions are far more devastating than what could have ever been imagined. Positionally speaking, the believer's flesh and its lusts were crucified at his or her conversion to Christ (Gal. 5:24). This fact teaches us about how God thinks of the flesh and about what He doesn't want in our lives. Because of this information, after regeneration, believers should continue to mortify the works of the flesh in their lives (Rom. 8:13; Col. 3:5) and to remove whatever provisions which would allow the flesh to lust (Rom. 6:11-12, 13:14). The flesh understands only two things: gratification and mortification. However, if we choose to gratify the flesh, even if only a little bit, it will want more the next day because the flesh is never satisfied – *"The eye is not satisfied with seeing, nor the ear filled with hearing"* (Eccl. 1:8). The only spiritual means of controlling the lusts of the flesh is to deal it a deadly blow and to keep on mortifying it day after day: this is the will of God.

Summary

Normally, when Scripture speaks of the will of God, it explicitly states what it is; there is no mystery about it, God has declared to us His general will for our lives. Consequently, the more pertinent question becomes, not what the will of God is for my life, but will I obey the revealed will of God for my life? If you are a believer in Christ there is only one right answer to this question. The Lord Jesus said, *"But why do you call Me 'Lord, Lord,' and not do the things which I say?"* (Luke 6:46), and *"If you love Me, keep My commandments"* (John 14:15).

> To walk out of God's will is to walk into nowhere.
>
> — C. S. Lewis

Obedience to the Lord Jesus practically proves our love for Him. A lack of love for the Lord will be shown through an unyielding spirit and through disobedience. There is such an intimate tie between genuine love for the Lord and obedience to the Lord that Paul bluntly states, *"If any man love not the Lord Jesus Christ, let him be Anathema* [eternally condemned]" (1 Cor. 16:22). Do you want to prove that you love the Lord Jesus Christ? Do you want to do the will of God in your life?

To answer "no" to either of these questions is the sin of pride; in effect, a "no" response is saying "I know more about what is right for my life than God does." To those who willfully reject God's revealed truth, Peter says, *"For it had been better for them not to have known the way of righteousness, than, after they have known it, to turn from the holy commandment delivered unto them"* (2 Peter 2:21). The more truth that is rejected, the more one's accountability with God is increased.

If the answer to these questions is "yes," the believer becomes better able to sense the leading of God into service; he or she becomes more cognizant of God's calling. God speaks to us in the quietness of His presence, so it is important that the

67

believer remove all hindrances to his or her communion with God – obedience is paramount (Ps. 66:18; Prov. 28:9).

> I find doing the will of God leaves me no time for disputing about His plans.
>
> — George MacDonald

The last time that the Lord Jesus spoke to His Father before the events of Calvary was in the Garden of Gethsemane, just before His arrest. The very last words Christ spoke to His Father until addressing Him from the cross were *"Your will be done"* (Matt. 26:42). God's will was done that day, although it cost the Lord everything, including His own life, to do it. The believer can do no better than to follow the Lord's example and do the will of God.

> To know the will of God is the greatest knowledge, to find the will of God is the greatest discovery, and to do the will of God is the greatest achievement.
>
> — George W. Truett

Girding the Mind for Service

Girding the mind refers to focusing our mental wherewithal on accomplishing an intended goal no matter what distractions, difficulties, or sufferings are encountered. In ancient days, the hulls of ships were undergirded with ropes and cables to keep them from breaking apart in storms (Acts 27:17). The girding of the ship strengthened it for the strenuous time ahead. Marathon runners comprehend the cost that the race will impose on their bodies. Runners mentally prepare (gird their minds) for the forthcoming pain and the exhaustion that will soon beset them in order to run with endurance and finish the race. This preparation enables runners not to be mentally distracted by cramping muscles, blisters, shin splints, cottonmouth, etc. – they run on for the prize; they run to finish the race well.

The matter of suffering patiently for the cause of Christ was very much a central theme in Peter's epistles. As mentioned earlier, he was writing to a group of scattered and persecuted Christians who were likely to experience more of the same. Peter encourages them: *"Therefore gird up the loins of your mind, be sober, and rest your hope fully upon the grace that is to be brought to you at the revelation of Jesus Christ"* (1 Pet. 1:13). William MacDonald provides the following comments concerning this verse:

> Peter urges the saints to have a "girded" mind. The girding up of the mind is an interesting figure of speech. In eastern lands, people wore long, flowing robes. When they wanted to walk fast or with a minimum of hindrance, they would tie the robe

69

up around their waist with a belt (see Ex. 12:11). In this way they girded up their loins. But what does Peter mean by gird up the loins of your mind? As they went out into a hostile world, believers were to avoid panic and distraction. In times of persecution, there is always the tendency to become rattled and confused. A girded mind is one that is strong, composed, cool, and ready for action. It is unimpeded by distraction of human fear or persecution.[1]

The matter of preparing His disciples for the arduous task ahead was very much on the mind of the Lord Jesus the night before He died. Much of the Lord's discourse with His disciples, as recorded in John 14 through 16, centers on this topic. After telling the disciples in John 13 that one of them was a betrayer, that Peter was going to deny Him, and that He was leaving them, the Lord provides a message of comfort in John 14. He informed them that after His departure the Comforter (the Holy Spirit) would come to them. The Lord also told them, *"I go to prepare a place for you. And if I go and prepare a place for you, I will come again and receive you to Myself; that where I am, there you may be also"* (John 14:2-3).

In John 15, the Lord tells them how to maintain fruitfulness – it is by abiding in Him. Through abiding in Christ a believer experiences the love of God (John 15:9), enjoys a powerful prayer-life (John 15:7), and experiences supernatural joy (John 15:11). John 15 contains the highest saturation of the word "hate" in all of Scripture. In the Greek passage, "hate" is found seven times and the word "world" occurs six times. However, the word "love" is found ten times in John 15 (this is the third highest chapter concentration of the word in any chapter of the Bible). It is interesting that all the occurrences of "hate" and "world" in the chapter are in or after verse 18 and all the occurrences of "love," "fruit," and "abide," except for a "love" in verse 19 are prior to verse 18. The message is this: The love of God, as demonstrated in the fruitful lives of believers, overcomes the hate of the world. The Lord clearly told His disciples what they should expect when serving Him so that they would not be depressed by the coming persecution:

> *If the world hates you, you know that it hated Me before it hated you. If you were of the world, the world would love its own. Yet because you are not of the world, but I chose you out of the world, therefore the world hates you. Remember the word that I said to you, 'A servant is not greater than his master.' If they persecuted Me, they will also persecute you* (John 15:18-20).

In John 16, the Lord Jesus summarized what He had been saying to His disciples that evening concerning suffering for Him, *"In the world you shall have tribulation: but be of good cheer; I have overcome the world"* (John 16:33). Follow Paul's example of using every troubling situation to magnify Christ and to further the cause of the gospel (Phil. 1:12, 20). Though a prisoner of Rome he chose to rejoice and to magnify Christ; as a result, the gospel penetrated into the heart of paganism and some in Caesar's own household were saved (Phil. 4:22). Paul understood that *"To live is Christ, and to die is gain."*

It is a promise of God that if you live to serve Christ you will suffer for it; dear believer, do not expect anything less and you will not be disappointed. Prepare your mind for the struggles ahead, and don't get bogged down in self-pity, grappling with despair when those forecasted storms of life arrive. If Christian in John Bunyan's *Pilgrim's Progress* had girded his mind, he would have likely avoided the "slough of despond." Every devoted Christian is destined for trouble, but not for despair: *"Yes, and all who desire to live godly in Christ Jesus will suffer persecution"* (2 Tim. 3:12). Every Christian that righteously suffers for the cause of Christ will be rewarded: *"If we suffer, we shall also reign with Him"* (2 Tim. 2:12, KJV).

Many years ago when the Bishop of Madras was visiting Travancore, there was introduced to him a little slave girl called "The Child Apostle." She had won this title by the zeal with

71

which she talked of Christ to others. Her quiet, steady persistence in this had won several converts to Christ. But she had suffered persecution too brutal to relate. When she was introduced to the Bishop, her face, neck, and arms were disfigured and scarred by stripes and blows. As he looked at her, the good man's eyes filled, and he said, "My child, how could you bear this?" She looked up at him in surprise and said, "Don't you like to suffer for Christ, sir?"[2]

Called to Serve

The previous chapters have discussed the preparatory work needed in a believer's life to better recognize God's call to ministry. Before anyone can know their calling in service, they must first trust Christ as Saviour. That individual then begins the divine process of sanctification in order to have the moral wherewithal to reflect Christ in his or her ministry. A believer is to search the Word of God to understand God's general will for his or her life, to work out gray areas, and to learn the heart of God. Believers need to understand the cost of discipleship: to serve God faithfully will result in persecution by the same world system that nailed the Lord Jesus to a cross. In this chapter, we will examine how to discern God's calling to service.

The Old Testament contains a number of examples of individuals who received direct instructions from God concerning their calling in life. God personally spoke to Abraham, Moses, Gideon, Samuel, Isaiah, Jeremiah, and Ezekiel to convey their calling. Saul, David, and Elisha received God's message for their lives from prophets. The means by which their callings were given are quite unique also: Abraham saw the God of glory, Samuel heard a still quiet voice, Isaiah and Ezekiel witnessed the majestic throne of God, and Moses bowed before a burning bush.

The New Testament also records the direct and specific calls of the disciples to ministry. So, how should a Christian today expect to understand God's personal call for him or her to serve? Should believers expect a voice from heaven, a vision, or a prophetic utterance to confirm God's calling for them? During the early days of the Church Age prophets were given to the Church as a check against false teachers – they confirmed the oral transmission of the Word of God before it was written down. Since believers have a divine anointing to understand truth (1 Jn. 2:20, 27) and the Word of God is now complete (Jude 3; 1 Cor. 13:9-10), modern Christians should not expect a prophetic confirmation of their ministry, at least in the normative sense. God may reveal Himself directly, but it should not be expected of Him to do so.

The fact is that the apostles, whom the Lord directly commissioned, have long since died, thus the apostolic age closed two millennia ago. This fact is also witnessed in Scripture in that the use of sign gifts (tongues, interpreting tongues, commanding miracles, etc.) steadily decreased in frequency as the New Testament was written. In fact, there is no recorded occurrence of these supernatural gifts after about 58 A.D., although over half of the New Testament was written after that time. The book of Acts reveals a clear transition from "apostles" to "apostles and elders" to just "elders" (speaking of local church leaders) through its record of early Church history. All of this is to say that today we should not expect specific revelation to confirm God's calling for us in ministry.

Practically speaking, how would you know a supernatural sign or a prophetic utterance was from God, anyway? It might be from the devil to lead you astray. Moreover, we tend to read into situations that which we want to be true – we are not very objective when we want something to be a certain way. For example, a young man once thought he was called by God to plant churches. After explaining this fact to a preacher, the preacher asked him, "How did you come to know your calling?" The young fellow said, "I was plowing in a field one day and saw two clouds floating overhead, one was shaped like a "P" and the other like a "C" and realized God wanted me to **p**lant **c**hurches. The preacher responded, "How do you know God wasn't telling you to 'plant corn'?" It is hard to be objective if we really want something to be a certain way.

A General Pattern

There is a general pattern of calling to service that is apparent in Scripture. In the life of David for example, three distinct stages of affirmation of his call as the leader of Israel are recorded:

> *Then all the tribes of Israel came to David at Hebron and spoke, saying, "Indeed we are your bone and your flesh. Also, in time past, when Saul was king over us, you were the one who led Israel out and brought them in; and the Lord said to you, 'You shall shepherd My people Israel, and be ruler over Israel.' "Therefore all the elders of Israel came to the king at Hebron, and King David made a covenant with them at Hebron before the Lord. And they anointed David king over Israel* (2 Sam. 5:1-3).

The southern kingdom (Judah) had recognized David as their king seven years earlier, thus David had been reigning over them in Hebron. Now the northern kingdom of Israel had decided to anoint David as their king also. What led them to this decision? First, they recognized that David had a divine calling; he had been personally selected by God for the purpose of ruling over them. Second, they recognized that it was David who led them in the practical affairs of the nation even when Saul was king. Given this understanding, they prudently recognized David as their king. David had a divine call, an internal call (i.e. he had an internal compulsion to do the work of leading), and then he was recognized by all.

When God plants a divine call into a person, with time and with proper spiritual maturity this calling becomes actively lived out in his or her life and others take notice. A believer often gains a sense of where he or she is going in ministry long before it happens – in some respects this can be a bit unsettling and may result in anxiety. In time, others will recognize what God is doing and validate the believer's call to service.

This three-stage process of calling is the same for elders (i.e. leaders in the local church): the Holy Spirit calls (appoints) them

(Acts 20:28), the internal call is shown by active service (1 Tim. 3:1), and eventually the serving shepherd will be morally and spiritual scrutinized according to the requirements of Titus 1 and 1 Timothy 3 and then be publicly recognized as an elder. God's working in the life of David and with church elders highlights the general way God calls and leads believers into the ministry He has chosen for them to accomplish.

The Call of Timothy

As mentioned previously, Scripture records Timothy's call to salvation, sanctification and service. There was no confusion as to what Timothy's call in ministry was to be as it was confirmed by prophetic utterance and was publicly announced through the laying on of hands (1 Tim. 4:12-16; 2 Tim. 1:6). Timothy had a distinct call into a unique discipleship ministry; he was often sent by Paul to follow up his pioneering efforts. Timothy would teach new converts sound doctrine and ensure that new assemblies adhered to proper Church order.

Prior to Timothy's specific call to service, Scripture records God's work to lead Timothy into his calling and to equip him for it. It is understood that God calls a minority of Christians into foreign mission fields or into full-time ministry service, yet He calls all believers to be faithful in their normal daily Christian experience. Every believer is called to do that which pleases the Lord each and every day. So whether you are an employee, a homemaker, a student, an elder or deacon in the Church, or a servant of others, endeavor to be faithful to what God has given you to do at this present time. Jim Elliot, who was martyred in Ecuador for the cause of Christ, put it this way: "Wherever you are, be all there." In Timothy's case, his faithfulness to the Lord in his day-to-day life prepared him to answer the call of a particular ministry later in life.

What do we know about Timothy prior to his ministry calling? We know that his mother and his grandmother were Jews and that his father was a Greek and that their hometown was

Lystra. Timothy was likely exposed to the gospel during Paul and Barnabas's first missionary trip into Asia Minor. Although Scripture does not record the exact timing of his conversion, the details in Acts and other epistles would indicate that he trusted Christ as a teenager, either directly through Paul's ministry or indirectly through others who heard the gospel through Paul. In any case, Paul considered Timothy to be his spiritual son, indicating he was likely connected in some way with his conversion.

Practically speaking, Timothy was one of the least-likely people for God to use in a ministry to both Jews and Greeks. His youth and his mixed ancestry would make it difficult for him to be accepted. Yet, this is the way God works: He acquires some unpromising material, He shapes, molds, and polishes a vessel so that it gleams with His grace, and then He uses it for His glory:

> *For you see your calling, brethren, that not many wise according to the flesh, not many mighty, not many noble, are called. But God has chosen the foolish things of the world to put to shame the wise, and God has chosen the weak things of the world to put to shame the things which are mighty; and the base things of the world and the things which are despised God has chosen, and the things which are not, to bring to nothing the things that are, that no flesh should glory in His presence* (1 Cor. 1:26-29).

Years ago, a veteran soldier relayed this story to me. He had been a truck driver before he enlisted in the Army and thought they would make him a truck driver because of his experience. However, to his shock, the Army made him a cook. When he complained that he didn't know anything about cooking, his commanding officer explained, "Good, you will learn to be a cook the Army way. If we made you a truck driver you would have driven trucks your way and not the Army way." God uses the least likely individuals to accomplish His work so that it gets done His way and all for His glory. The Lord already knows all about our strengths and weaknesses and His grace will overcome both, especially our strengths.

So if you feel like you are the least likely person God might use for some spectacular ministry, don't be surprised if you are the one called to do it. If so, you are blessed in that you will never question whether or not God's will was done. The lack of natural ability to accomplish some feat for the Lord means the reception of supernatural help. God is more concerned with your availability than with your ability; the latter just promotes pride anyway.

Timothy had taken obvious steps in readying himself for service. In examining his life, I find four distinct activities which led Timothy into his service calling, which at some point in his life was also confirmed by prophetic announcement.

Step One

The first step in preparing for ministry is recorded in 2 Timothy 3:14-15 where Paul acknowledges that Timothy had grown in the Scriptures and that this had equipped him for every good work:

> *But you must continue in the things which you have learned and been assured of, knowing from whom you have learned them, and that from childhood you have known the Holy Scriptures, which are able to make you wise for salvation through faith which is in Christ Jesus. All Scripture is given by inspiration of God, and is profitable for doctrine, for reproof, for correction, for instruction in righteousness,* **that the man of God may be complete, thoroughly equipped for every good work** *(2 Tim. 3:14-17).*

Before his conversion, his mother and grandmother had taught Timothy the Old Testament. Later, Paul revealed New Testament truth to him. He would go on to teach others what he himself had learned from God's Word. Timothy understood that knowing God's Word was essential in order to be prepared for service. As stated earlier, God speaks to us in the secret of His presence; therefore, we must be consistently in His Word to know His leading in our lives.

Step Two

Not only had Timothy grown in his knowledge of Scripture, he had grown spiritually also, a matter that others readily testified of: *"He was well spoken of by the brethren who were at Lystra and Iconium"* (Acts 16:2). Some five years had passed since Paul first visited Lystra; now he and Silas were passing through the area again. In the interim between his visits, Timothy had become well-known to the believers, not only in his hometown, but also in Iconium, which was some twenty miles from Lystra. For a young man to be so well-reported within this region could only mean one thing: he had proven himself faithful to the Lord's people in service. Timothy was publicly recognized for his ministry to others and was commended to Paul because of it.

Additionally, Timothy had a wholesome testimony; in fact, his name means "honoring God." The term "man of God" is used only twice in the New Testament and both times it is used to directly or indirectly refer to Timothy (1 Tim. 6:11; 2 Tim. 3:17). So impressed was Paul with Timothy's growth and purity that he desired that he join the missionary team. This was a great opportunity for learning and gaining practical experience, and Timothy agreed to go.

In application, every believer should be faithful to complete whatever responsibilities he or she has already been assigned before desiring or expecting additional opportunities to serve the Lord:

> *Let every man abide in the same calling wherein he was called. Art thou called being a servant? care not for it: but if thou mayest be made free, use it rather. For he that is called in the Lord, being a servant, is the Lord's freeman: likewise also he that is called, being free, is Christ's servant. Ye are bought with a price; be not ye the servants of men. Brethren,*

let every man, wherein he is called, therein abide with God (1 Cor. 7:20-24).

The Lord provides greater opportunities for service as His people are faithful to what they have already been asked to do (Luke 16:10-11). I find no example in Scripture where the Lord called a lazy person to serve Him. Elisha was plowing behind twelve yoke of oxen when he received his call from Elijah. Moses and David were shepherding sheep when God beckoned them to service. Gideon was summoned while threshing wheat. Four of the disciples were fishing when they were told by the Lord Jesus, "Follow Me." The Lord calls working people to serve Him.

A young woman told a well-known preacher that she felt God had called her to the mission field of Africa. The preacher responded, "I doubt that is the case." The woman was distraught and exclaimed, "But you don't know how I have agonized over this decision!" With more gentleness, the preacher explained his initial response, "My dear, I know for a fact that you are not faithful in helping your mother keep the home. Why then would God call you to greater responsibility when you have not determined to serve Him faithfully in what He has already given you to do?" The home and local assembly provide wonderful opportunities to learn discipline and to demonstrate faithfulness to God. Dear believer, be faithful in whatever ministry God has given you and don't be startled if in response to your faithfulness the Lord extends to you even greater privileges to serve Him. The following story is taken from the life of Harry Ironside and illustrates this point.

Harry Ironside, when a boy, helped his widowed mother by working during vacations, Saturdays, and out-of-school for a Scottish shoeworker who was a Christian. He posted Bible verses all over the shop so that everywhere one looked, he would see the Word of God. No package went out to a customer without a tract or a word of testimony, and many came back for salvation. Harry's job was to pound leather for shoe soles. A piece of cowhide was cut to size, soaked in water, and pounded until it was hard and dry. After endless poundings, he was weary. One day, he noticed that another godless cobbler was not pounding, but was nailing the soles while still wet. "So they come back quicker," was the reply. Ironside discussed this practice with his Christian owner who responded: "I do not cobble just for 50¢ or 75¢ from customers. I do it for the glory of God. In heaven, I expect every shoe returned to me in a pile, and I do not want the Lord to say, "Dan, that was a poor job. You did not do your best."[1]

We labor to please the Lord and no one else; remembering this will guard our heart against pride and our minds from seeking and justifying an easier path.

Step Three

Timothy was mentored and guided by older men. There are many scriptural examples which indicate the Lord often yokes the energy and zeal of younger servants with the wisdom and knowledge of older ones. Moses and Joshua labored together for forty years before their separation at the Jordan River. Elijah mentored and served with Elisha for approximately ten years before Elijah was taken up to heaven by a fiery chariot.

Barnabas ventured from Antioch to Tarsus in order to bring Paul back to Antioch with him (Acts 11:25-26). Initially, Barnabas mentored Paul and assisted his growth, but by Acts 13 (perhaps two years later) they were clearly working together as peers, and by the end of that chapter, we read for the first time of "Paul and Barnabas" (v. 46) instead of "Barnabas and Paul." The pupil had exceeded his mentor in the speaking aspects of their missionary ministry. Later, Barnabas would mentor John Mark and see him restored to fruitfulness (he had withdrawn from missionary service earlier in his life).

It is evident that God used older servants of His to confirm Timothy's calling and to assist him in fulfilling it. Shortly after

Timothy departed from Lystra to join the missionary team, we read the following (several pronouns and verbs are identified by bold text for emphasis):

> *Now when they had gone through Phrygia and the region of Galatia, **they were** forbidden by the Holy Spirit to preach the word in Asia. **After they** had come to Mysia, **they tried** to go into Bithynia, but the Spirit did not permit **them**. So passing by Mysia, **they came** down to Troas. And a vision appeared **to Paul** in the night. A man of Macedonia stood and pleaded with him, saying, "Come over to Macedonia and help us." Now **after he** had seen the vision, **immediately we** sought to go to Macedonia, concluding **that the Lord had called us** to preach the gospel to them* (Acts 16:6-10).

Though the team labored together to proclaim the gospel, it was the veteran missionary that received direction from the Lord. Paul's call became the call of all those with him. So initially, Paul mentored and guided Timothy in ministry, but later, they co-labored as peers for the cause of Christ. This working relationship lasted some twenty years and is a wonderful testimony of the grace of God in their lives.

Please note that Timothy was called to a ministry and not a location. The book of Acts records the fact that the Lord's servants rarely remained in one location for very long. Aquila and Priscilla were used first in Corinth, then in Ephesus, then at Rome, and then again in Ephesus to disciple Christians and start local church gatherings. According to Scripture, Paul's two and half year stay in Ephesus was the longest period of time he spent serving in one location. As a principle, this example is contrary to the *resident worker* pattern which prevails in Christianity today.

The pattern of older saints mentoring and equipping younger ones for service is a biblical example and forms the foundation of discipleship – the means in which Christ builds His Church. Towards the end of his life, Paul clearly affirms this mentoring/equipping protocol with his spiritual son Timothy:

You therefore, my son, be strong in the grace that is in Christ Jesus. And the things that you have heard from me among many witnesses, commit these to faithful men who will be able to teach others also (2 Tim. 2:1-2).

Paul notes four generations of disciples: himself, Timothy, faithful men, and those whom the faithful men would teach. Mentoring and equipping one for ministry and confirming one's ability and calling are spiritual blessings which older saints can extend to younger ones in the Lord. In application, it would be good for those who seriously want to serve the Lord to seek out veteran servants for counsel, assistance, and mentoring. Additionally, it would be wise to remain in good fellowship with the elders in your local assembly; these men have God's authority to lead and protect you (Heb. 13:7, 17, 24).

Unfortunately, this pattern cannot be discussed without offering a warning. I praise God for visionaries; they are a unique gift to the Church and enable us to see what could be and motivate us to "think outside the box." With this said, it has also been my observation that visionaries tend to avoid accountability and typically surround themselves with "yes men" to ensure they have a free hand. Without godly counsel and good accountability a visionary may become an *agendary* who adapts an "end justifies the means" mentality, the result of which ultimately hurts God's people. Elegant wit, clever anecdotes, and trenchant speech should not be used to overwhelm, mesmerize or control younger believers. Babes in Christ must be taught sound doctrine and should receive ministry guidance, but they should not be cajoled by heavy-handed tactics or hoodwinked for personal gain.

Yes, veteran soldiers of the cross are needed to mentor younger believers, but only if their lives are consistent with the Word of God. Sound doctrine is not merely "head knowledge" – it is lived out (Titus 2:1); so if you are a younger believer looking for guidance, enlist the help of only those who are consistently living sound doctrine. Their home-life, social-life, and church-life will testify of either real spirituality, or what is merely a superficial façade. Sound doctrine is lived out by the grace of God; it cannot by fabricated by human effort!

Step Four

Though Paul was instrumental in affirming Timothy's call to service, Timothy himself became aware of his calling through doing the work and seeing God's blessing. Even though his young age and the peril of the work weighed on his mind, his ministry was a huge blessing to others and, therefore, obviously had God's endorsement. Though Timothy didn't know all that God had called him to do in the beginning, he was faithful to what God had revealed to him and in time God gave him further ministry confirmation and direction.

Paul desired the Church at Philippi to have his same aspiration for serving Christ: *"I press toward the goal for the prize of the upward call of God in Christ Jesus"* (Phil. 3:14), but he also realized that many younger saints would not understand what he was talking about. Paul offered them this advice, *"Therefore let us, as many as are mature, have this mind; and **if in anything you think otherwise, God will reveal even this to you**. Nevertheless, **to the degree that we have already attained, let us walk by the same rule**, let us be of the same mind"* (Phil. 3:15-16).

Dear believer, you may not understand where the Lord is leading you at this present moment, but keep pressing on for the upward call of God in Christ Jesus. Be faithful to what you know to be true; maturity (and the confirmation of your calling) will come in time. Remember, God grows ministries as He grows people. While in this early growing-phase of ministry be faithful to what you know regarding your calling and long for what is yet to be revealed. Here are a few questions to ask yourself to help in discerning the mind of the Lord and in confirming God's direction for your life.

Is God blessing my ministry or am I hurting the Church?

Do I receive joy when serving the Lord in a particular way more than in other ways?

Am I burdened for a ministry or burdened by it?

Am I growing in Christ likeness as I serve in a particular ministry?

Is the Lord opening new opportunities in a particular area of service?

Do senior saints (because of their broader experience base) have unified feedback about your ministry?

Believers are not perfect, so don't be discouraged if you explore an area of service and it doesn't go anywhere. It may not be the ministry that God has called you into, it may have been a preparatory work that the Lord wanted you to experience in order to be ready for something else, or it may not be the right timing. When the Lord opens the doors of a ministry, no one can close them (Rev. 3:7). When the Lord closes the doors of ministry, He usually opens others (this assumes that sin was not the cause of the discontinued ministry).

The first attempt of David Livingstone to preach ended in failure: "Friends, I have forgotten all I had to say," he gasped, and in shame stepped from the pulpit! At that moment, Robert Moffat, who was visiting Edinburgh at that time, advised David not to give up. Perhaps Livingstone could be a doctor instead of a preacher, he advised. Livingstone decided to be both, and when his years of medical study were done he went to Africa.[2]

Proverbs 24:16 reads, *"For a righteous man may fall seven times and rise again, but the wicked shall fall by calamity."* It is not falling that makes a believer a failure – it is staying down. Falling is a natural part of learning to walk, so let us learn from our mistakes and by the grace of God rise from the ground and keep walking.

Answer the Call

Dear believer, be *"confident of this very thing, that He who has begun a good work in you will complete it until the day of Jesus Christ"* (Phil. 1:6-7). *"For we are His workmanship, created in Christ Jesus for good works, which God prepared beforehand that we should walk in them"* (Eph. 2:10). God is sovereign and will preserve us in this world until our homecoming. Until that time, may we diligently co-labor with Him (1 Cor. 3:9) in those things that He has prepared for us to do in order to honor Him.

Equipped to Serve

When God called young Jeremiah, the son of a priest, to be His prophet, no doubt Jeremiah was thinking it would be much easier to serve the Lord as a priest. Offering sacrifices to the Lord in the temple was something he already knew about; besides this, the occupation was socially admired – preaching God's judgment to a stiff-necked people was an entirely different matter. He was the son of a priest and that would normally mean his calling in life would be to offer up worship to God on behalf of the nation. But God was not interested in receiving worship from His idolatrous people; rather, the time had come to chasten them. The ministry of a prophet, a spokesman for God, was more necessary than that of a priest.

Despite his youth, the difficult task, and the hazardous social situation, Jeremiah accepted God's call for his life. He was honest with God about his own deficiencies, but he also knew that God was greater than those weaknesses and would enable him to accomplish the task at hand. In fact, the Lord touched Jeremiah's mouth and put His words there (Jer. 1:9), and then He promised him that he would carry His message to the nations (Jer. 1:10). This message was indeed dangerous, but God was with Jeremiah and the Lord would fulfill His promise to protect him (Jer. 1:9).

The Lord Jesus *"called His twelve disciples together and gave them power and authority over all demons, and to cure diseases. He sent them to preach the kingdom of God and to heal the sick"* (Luke 9:1-2). After an undisclosed interval of time we read, *"And the apostles, when they had returned, told Him all that they had done"* (Luke 9:10). The Lord Jesus called and sent out His disciples into Galilee to preach the kingdom gospel message. He did not send them out without uniquely equipping them for the task; they received authority and power from Him. The exercise of this authority, by faith, would enable their ministry to be empowered by God. Indeed, the disciples were able to do wonderful miracles in the performance of their ministry, their only limitation was their faith (Luke 9:40-41).

Saul, later named Paul, was on his way to Damascus to imprison Christians when he had a close encounter with the Lord Jesus that led to his conversion. After Paul obeyed the Lord's command to go into Damascus and to wait there for further instructions, the Lord sent Ananias to him. Ananias confirmed God's calling for Saul: *"He is a chosen vessel of Mine to bear My name before Gentiles, kings, and the children of Israel. For I will show him how many things he must suffer for My name's sake"* (Acts 9:15-16).

How would you respond to a divine commission such as Paul's? As a new convert, he was told that his calling would result in much personal suffering. Without God's enablement, such a call would be overwhelming, especially given Saul's remorse over his previous imprisonment of Christians and his consenting to their death. Yet, Paul later acknowledged what enabled him to be an overcomer and to obey his calling:

> *For I am the least of the apostles, who am not worthy to be called an apostle, because I persecuted the church of God. But by the grace of God I am what I am, and His grace toward me was not in vain; but I labored more abundantly than they all, yet not I, but the grace of God which was with me* (1 Cor. 15:9-10).

When a believer chooses to obey God's calling for his or her life, God will always equip and enable that individual to successfully answer the call. Whether called to serve in the home as a wife and mother, or as the treasurer of a local church, or as a nurse in a field hospital, or as a missionary in a foreign field – God provides ample grace to accomplish the ministry.

Hudson Taylor, a pioneer missionary into China in the mid-nineteenth century had two important sayings on this matter. First, "God always gives his very best to those who leave the choice with him."[1] Second, quoting the missionary Anthony Norris Groves, Taylor said, "When God's work is done in God's way for God's glory, it will not lack for God's supply."[2] This is especially true in times of ministry crisis. Hudson Taylor noted that every time there had been a wonderful expansion of the missionary work in China it had been preceded by a time of deep trial. The Lord enables His people both to suffer for Him and to serve Him, if they will remain faithful to Him. Faith forged in fiery trials is made stronger than it was before.

The Lord Jesus told His disciples that they would face some challenging days ahead; however, that was not the end of His message:

> *You will be brought before governors and kings for My sake, as a testimony to them and to the Gentiles. But when they deliver you up, do not worry about how or what you should speak. For it will be given to you in that hour what you should speak; for it is not you who speak, but the Spirit of your Father who speaks in you* (Matt. 10:18-20).

When a ministry is a true work of God and its minister is truly doing the work of God there will be no lack of God's enablement for both. The believer must be faithful to his or her calling and must learn to trust the Lord for wisdom and grace in every situation. Faith that is not tested will not be trusted; trials, therefore, become a necessary part of any ministry.

Take Up Your Cross

We have been thinking together for several chapters about God's calls to salvation, to sanctification, and to service. All three calls are integrally connected, require human responsibility, and form God's sovereign plan for our lives. Each believer is a unique work of God and the way He works with each of us is unique also. The paramount question is how far will we go on with the Lord? How willing are we to answer His calling for our lives?

When teaching His disciples about discipleship, the Lord Jesus said:

> *If anyone desires to come after Me, let him deny himself, and take up his cross daily, and follow Me. For whoever desires to save his life will lose it, but whoever loses his life for My sake will save it. For what profit is it to a man if he gains the whole world, and is himself destroyed or lost? (Luke 9:23-25).*

Many come to Christ's cross for salvation but then neglect to go on with Him and bear their own cross; this is an affront to the discipleship message He taught. The believer was never to flee the cross, but rather is to die daily upon it – only then does his or her life count for eternity. As mentioned previously, this was the lesson Peter learned; he found that it was harder to live for Christ and die daily, than to just die once as a martyr. The believer must, practically speaking, die for the life of Christ to be lived out, as A. W. Tozer explains:

If we are wise, we will do what Jesus said: endure the cross and despise its shame for the joy that is set before us. To do this is to submit the whole pattern of our life to be destroyed and built again in the power of an endless life. And we shall find that it is more than poetry, more than sweet hymnody and elevated feeling. The cross will cut into our lives where it hurts worst, sparing neither us nor our carefully cultivated reputation. It will defeat us and bring our selfish life to an end.[1]

Billy Graham summarizes the matter of the believer's cross concisely: "To take up the cross means that you take your stand for the Lord Jesus no matter what it costs."[2] The following three testimonies are of individuals who decided to dedicate themselves fully to Christ and obey His calling for their lives no matter what the personal cost would be. Their obedience ultimately determined how they would die, which as A. W. Tozer explains is the natural outcome of cross-bearing:

The man with a cross no longer controls his destiny; he lost control when he picked up his cross. That cross immediately became to him an all-absorbing interest, an overwhelming interference. No matter what he may desire to do, there is but one thing he can do; that is, move on toward the place of crucifixion.[3]

The Lord Jesus is a gentleman; He will not force you to bear your cross or obey His calling for your life, but not to do so is in direct violation of His will. To ignore His calling is to have an existence which has no meaning and no eternal value. Such a miserable existence is nothing more than a salute to the delusional lies of Satan. May the Lord speak to you in a personal way as you read these testimonies and contemplate the value of a life spent for Christ.

C. T. Studd

At the age of 16, C. T. Studd was already an expert cricket player and at nineteen, he was appointed the captain of his team at Eton, England. Soon he became a world-famous sports personality. But the Lord had different plans for him, for while attending Cambridge University he heard D. L. Moody preach and was wondrously saved. He soon dedicated his life and his inherited wealth to Christ and spent hours seeking to convert his teammates. Sensing God's leading to full-time service, he offered himself to Hudson Taylor for missionary work in China.

While in that foreign country, he inherited a sum of money equivalent today to several million dollars. Within twenty-four hours he gave the entire inheritance away, investing it in the things of the Lord. Later, he was forced to go back to England because his health was failing and his wife was an invalid. But God called him again—this time to the heart of Africa. He was informed that if he went he would not live long. His only answer was that he had been looking for a chance to die for Jesus. "Faithful unto death," he accepted God's call and labored in Africa until the Saviour took him home in 1931.[4]

> Some wish to live within the sound of church and chapel bell. I wish to run a rescue mission within a yard of hell.
>
> — C. T. Studd

Jim Elliot

Another young man, Jim Elliot, was also determined to live his life for Christ regardless of the personal cost. On January 8, 1956, Elliot was one of the five missionaries speared to death by Auca Indians at the Curaray River in Ecuador: he was 28 years old, Peter Fleming was 27, Ed McCully was 28, Roger Youderian was 31, and Nate Saint was 32.

In 1959, Nate Saint's sister, Rachel, and Jim Elliot's widow, Elisabeth, made contact with this fierce tribe. Rachel Saint remained with them for 30 years. These women were instrumental in leading the actual killers of their loved ones to Christ, effectively ending generations of tribal revenge killings, which in recent years had wiped out 60 percent of the tribe.[5]

James Boster, an anthropologist from the University of Connecticut, studied the history of Auca revenge murders and concluded that Christian conversion prevented self-extinction (The tribe had dwindled down to 600 members in 1958, but at present it numbers about 2,000.). He notes:

> Deadly cycles of revenge had scattered them into small, paranoid factions. Attempted truces failed because their language had no words for abstractions such as "peace." Because Christianity was brought by kin of men they had killed, but who befriended them in return, it became a powerful way to signal commitment to nonviolence.[6]

In a journal entry, Jim Elliot wrote, "God, I pray Thee, light these idle sticks of my life, that I may burn for Thee. Consume my life, my God, for it is Thine. I seek not a long life, but a full one, like You, Lord Jesus." Two years later, he wrote, "I must not think it strange if God takes in youth those whom I would have kept on earth till they were older. God is peopling Eternity, and I must not restrict Him to old men and women."[7]

> He is no fool to give what he cannot keep, to gain what he cannot lose.
>
> — Jim Elliot

David Livingstone

David Livingstone, a contemporary of Hudson Taylor, was divinely called to bring the gospel message to the interior of Africa, a missionary field into which no other white man had dared to venture. For decades, he hazarded his life exploring the perilous jungles of Africa often while suffering from a malaria flare up. He successfully trekked some 30,000 to 40,000 miles through the interior of Africa before his death, all the while preaching the gospel of Jesus Christ to the natives (many of whom were cannibals), and mapping the interior of Africa. He had hoped that his exploration and careful documentation would establish trade routes that would assist in ending the slave trade.

After these years of adversity, he was found dead in the simplest of living conditions: a grass hut furnished only with a bed, a desk and a chair. His body was brought back to England, where a funeral service was held at Westminster Abbey and all of England honored this brave missionary. Livingstone's Bible was found alongside his body and examination of it revealed that the ink was nearly worn off of Psalm 46. In that Psalm we read, *"The Lord of hosts is with us; the God of Jacob is our refuge"* and *"God is our refuge and strength, a very present help in trouble!"* Livingstone had etched his own record of trust upon the holy page by passing his finger repeatedly over the text. What was it that had brought him peace in the midst of the danger and the unforeseen trials that had constantly challenged his resolve? It was knowing the presence and the peace of Christ.

Towards the end of his life, David Livingstone wrote this concerning a life lived for Christ:

> People talk of the sacrifice I have made in spending so much of my life in Africa. Can that be called a sacrifice which is simply paid back as a small part of the great debt owed to our God, which we can never repay? Is that a sacrifice which brings its own reward of healthful activity, the consciousness of doing good, peace of mind, and a bright hope of a glorious destiny hereafter?

> Away with such a word, such a view, and such a thought! It is emphatically no sacrifice. Say rather it is a privilege. Anxiety, sickness, suffering or danger now and then, with a foregoing of the common conveniences and charities of this life, may make us pause and cause the spirit to waver and sink; but let this only be for a moment. All these are nothing when compared with the glory which shall hereafter be revealed in and for us. I never made a sacrifice. Of this we ought not to talk when we remember the great sacrifice which He made who left His Father's throne on high to give Himself for us.[8]

— David Livingstone

A Cloud of Witnesses

After identifying a number of individuals in the Bible who pleased God by exercising faith in His Word, the writer of Hebrews drew his teaching on faith to a close with this exhortation:

> *Therefore we also, since we are surrounded by so great a cloud of witnesses, let us lay aside every weight, and the sin which so easily ensnares us, and let us run with endurance the race that is set before us, looking unto Jesus, the author and finisher of our faith, who for the joy that was set before Him endured the cross, despising the shame, and has sat down at the right hand of the throne of God. For consider Him who endured such hostility from sinners against Himself, lest you become weary and discouraged in your souls* (Heb. 12:1-3).

The writer referred back to the previously mentioned faithfulness of Old Testament saints to motivate believers at that time to remain faithful to the Lord. Concerning this *great cloud of witnesses*, William MacDonald writes: "This does not mean that they are spectators of what goes on on earth. Rather they witness to us by their lives of faith and endurance and set a high standard for us to duplicate."[9] Not just the Old Testament saints mentioned in Hebrews, but a great cloud of witnesses throughout the Church Age also encourage believers at this present time to keep their eyes affixed on Christ, to be faithful to Him, and to run with patience until each one's course is finished. Their devotion to God is a legacy not soon to be forgotten and their rallying cries continue to resound in our ears:

George Whitefield, the famous English evangelist: "O Lord, give me souls, or take my soul!"

David Brainerd, missionary to the North American Indians: "Lord, to Thee I dedicate myself. O accept me and let me be Thine forever. Lord, I desire nothing else. I desire nothing more." His last diary entry, "O Come, Lord Jesus, come quickly. Amen." He died at the age of 29.

John Wesley: "Give me 100 preachers who fear nothing but sin and desire nothing but God, and I care not a straw whether they be clergy or laymen, such alone will shake the gates of hell."

William Carey, a pioneer missionary to India: "To know the will of God, we need an open Bible and an open map."

Dwight L. Moody: "Use me then, my Saviour, for whatever purpose and in whatever way Thou mayest require. Here is my poor heart an empty vessel; fill it with Thy grace."

John McKenzie in contemplation of being a missionary prayed while kneeling on the banks of the Lossie: "O Lord, send me to the darkest spot on earth!"

Gladys Aylward, missionary to China, "I wasn't God's first choice for what I've done for China. I don't know who it was... It must have been a man... a well-educated man. I don't know what happened. Perhaps he died. Perhaps he wasn't willing... And God looked down and saw Gladys Aylward and God said, "Well, she's willing."

"Praying Hyde," a missionary in India: "Father, give me these souls, or I die."

John Hunt, a missionary to the Fiji Islands, prayed upon his deathbed: "Lord, save Fiji, save Fiji, save these people, O Lord; have mercy upon Fiji; save Fiji!"

Nate Saint, martyr in Ecuador: "People who do not know the Lord ask why in the world we waste our lives as missionaries. They forget that they too are expending their lives ... and when the bubble has burst, they will have nothing of eternal significance to show for the years they have wasted."

Amy Carmichael, missionary to India: "The saddest thing one meets is a nominal Christian."

The Challenge

God summons believers to many types of ministries, some in the home, some in the local assembly, some in the work place, and some in mission fields. All are important in God's plan. As an example, the ministries of John and Charles Wesley were made possible because their mother, Susanne, trained them up for the Lord and upheld them in prayer. Susanne proved the saying, "The hand that rocks the cradle is the hand that rules the world" to be true.

For our lives to have meaning and significance in God's plan we must personally answer His calls of salvation, of sanctification, and of service. Each divine call of God is distinctive, yet collectively they represent God's will for our lives. As individuals yield to God's calling they experience and enjoy the progressive work of God in their lives. Each time we respond by faith to God's summons the result is always spiritual promotion (e.g. we become a child of God, we develop Christ-like character, we learn more of God, or we become fruitful in ministry). We discover both the meaning and the purpose of life by answering God's call.

So how about you; when God weighs out the value of your life in His infallible scales, will it count for eternity or count for nothing? Before the opportunity to experience a meaningful life is lost, answer God's call for your life – you will never regret it!

Endnotes

Preface
1. P. L. Tan, *Encyclopedia of 7700 illustrations* (Bible Communications, Garland TX; 1996, c1979)
2. Oswald Chambers, *My Utmost for His Highest* – Jan. 17th

A Promotion Offer
1. Edythe Draper, *Draper's Quotations from the Christian World* (Tyndale House Pub. Inc., Wheaton, IL – electronic copy)
2. William MacDonald, True Discipleship (Walterick Pub., Kansas City, KS; 1975), p. 56
3. P.L. Tan, op. cit.

Name Calling
1. W. Grinton Berry, *Foxe's Book of Martyrs* (Power Books, Old Tappen, New Jersey), p. 9

Come Out!
1. R. P. Amos, *The Church* (Every Day Publications Inc., Port Colborne, ON; 2006), p. 7
2. Edythe Draper, op. cit.
3. Alexander Hislop, *The Two Babylons* (Loizeaux Brothers, Neptune, NJ; 2nd ed. – 1959), p. 21
4. Ibid., p. 22
5. Ibid., p. 69
6. Ibid., p. 21
7. Ibid., p. 87
8 Ibid., p. 62
9. Ibid., p. 69
10. Edythe Draper, op. cit.
11. Ibid.

Doing the Will of God
1. Ibid.

Doing the Will of God (cont.)
2. P.L. Tan, op. cit.
3. Edythe Draper, op. cit.
4. www.bible.ca/ef/topical-robbed-broke-but-thankful.htm
5. Dr. Howard Taylor, *Spiritual Secret of Hudson Taylor* (Whitaker House, New Kensington, PA: 1996), p. 273
6. Ibid., p. 275
7. Ibid., p. 282
8. Edythe Draper, op. cit.
9. Ibid.
10. P.L. Tan, op. cit.
11. Ibid.
12. Ibid.

Girding the Mind for Service
1. William MacDonald, *Believer's Bible Commentary* (Thomas Nelson Publishers, Nashville, TN: 1989), p. 2254
2. P.L. Tan, op. cit.

Called to Serve
1. Ibid.
2. Ibid.

Equipped to Serve
1. Edythe Draper, op. cit.
2. Warren Wiersbe, *Be Joyful: A New Testament Study – Philippians* (Victor Books, Wheaton, Il; 1996 – electronic copy)

Take Up Your Cross
1. Edythe Draper, op. cit.
2. Ibid.
3. Ibid.
4. P.L. Tan, op. cit.
5. http://www.nationmaster.com/encyclopedia/Huaorani
6. http://www.post-gazette.com/pg/06008/633940.stm
7. P.L. Tan, op. cit.
8. Ibid.
9. William MacDonald, *Believer's Bible Commentary*, op. cit., p. 2202

Suggested Reading
God's Call to Special Service by T. E. Wilson
The Training of the Twelve by Alexander B. Bruce

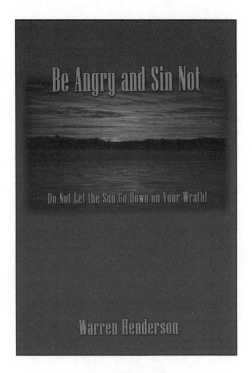

Be Angry and Sin Not
Warren Henderson
B-7051

From Scripture, we will learn of God's holy anger, then commence upon the difficult task of aligning our selfish anger and unrighteous behavior with His righteousness. This task will require each of us to honestly evaluate our anger tendencies, to remove internal conditions that frequently induce angry feelings, and to learn techniques to mange our anger in a God-honoring way. If you mismanage anger, this book will guide you into better self-control. Be Angry And Sin Not tackles such questions as,

> * Why am I angry?
> * Should I be angry?
> * How do I control my angry feelings?
> * How can my anger benefit others and serve God?

The Fruitful Vine
Warren Henderson
B-7132

The Fruitful Vine contains six sections. The first, The Marital Union, supplies the biblical foundation for the remainder of the book: Why was marriage instituted, and what was God's best plan for marriage? The chapter "To Marry or Not?" offers guidance and encouragement to unmarried women, both those called to "singleness" and those "maids in waiting." The following three sections pertain to the natural roles a married woman will find the most joy in fulfilling - namely, being a companion to her husband, bearing and nurturing children, and keeping an ordered home. The fifth section, The Autumn Years, provides counsel to the "empty-nesters" and encouragement for widows. The final section provides a character sketch of a spiritually-minded woman and the types of ministry she may engage in. Through Scripture, God has revealed both what He finds beautiful in a woman and what He expects of her.

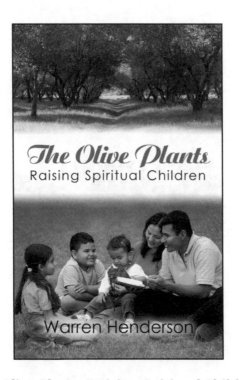

Olive Plants: Raising Spiritual Children
Warren Henderson
B-7514

Most of the Christian children's ministry today is aimed at raising "moral" children. The teaching of right and wrong is necessary, but this agenda will fall pitifully short of producing "spiritual" children. Children must develop morally, physically, spiritually, emotionally, and academically, to really thrive and reach God's full potential for their lives. When children have a balanced development they lay hold of self-acceptance and self-awareness of their calling in God's master plan. In so doing, they gain a sense of importance and security-God is in control and has a plan for my life.

"Wisdom is something that all parents gain over time, some more than others, and some later than others, and for these the learning is often accompanied by frustration and sorrow. It is our earnest prayer that this resource will alleviate parents from experiencing the latter situation." —Warren Henderson

Hallowed Be Thy Name
Warren Henderson
B-7450

Is scriptural terminology important? Does wrong terminology tend to lead to erroneous Church practices? Do I ignorantly show disdain for the Lord's name by the way in which I address Him or speak of Him to others? What is the sin of blasphemy? Can a Christian blaspheme God today? These are some of the questions Hallowed Be Thy Name examines in detail. Our speech and behaviour reflect our heart's adoration for the Lord Jesus and, thus, directly affect our testimony of Him to the world. May God bestow us grace to *"buy the truth, and sell it not"* (Prov. 23:23), and may each one be subject to the *"good, and acceptable, and perfect, will of God"* (Rom. 12:2).